CHRISTOPHER DESANTIS

wicked
books

A NOVEL

NOVEMBER
PRESS

ISBN-13: 978-0-6151-5480-0

www.christopherdesantis.com

Jacket and overall publication design by Greg deSantis

Made in the USA

For my family.

CONTENTS

WICK-ED [wik'id] adj.
morally bad; evil
generally bad, unpleasant, etc.
[Slang] showing great skill and prowess; awesome.

Prologue:
FOXFIELD, MASS

Far up the eastern seaboard, past the noisy traffic in the streets of Boston and beyond the gangs of tourists visiting the autumn foliage, rests the sleepy little town of Foxfield, Massachusetts.

Strangely enough, there are no foxes in the town of Foxfield, and for that matter there is no field. There used to be a field, a vast ocean of tall grass and cattails, but it vanished a long time ago, as did all of the foxes.

Some say the field disappeared when the forest started to grow wild. Overnight the woodlands exploded in a mass of twisted branches and prickly thorns. The trees shot up to enormous heights, blotting out the sky with a thick canopy of leaves. Bushes and shrubs began to grow in the strangest of places, popping out of people's cupboards, and filling whole garages. Tree trunks burst their way through living room floors, causing roofs to collapse under the weight of their enormous knotted branches, while massive vines crept their way from the forest's edge and wrapped themselves around the town folk's cars like giant boa constrictors. The roads were blocked, the stores had to close, and the people were forced to leave.

The residents of Foxfield aren't certain what caused the forest to become so ravenous. It just continued to grow and grow until all that was left untouched was the town common and the old bronze statue of Foxfield's colonial founder, Jacob Smalls. So the people decided to leave their ruined homes behind and rebuild their community on the edge of the woodlands, far from the center of the forest where the statue of Jacob rested. There they rebuilt their homes and their lives.

Nobody knows what became of the foxes.

Chapter One:
GABRIEL WOODS

"Are you still in bed?" Mrs. Woods asked as she entered Gabriel's bedroom and flung the blinds wide with a yank of the faded nylon cord. The glaring light of the morning sun blasted through the dirty window pane and stung Gabriel's eyes.

Gabriel Woods sat up in bed and rubbed his eyes with the palms of his hands. His pajamas (if you could call hand-me-down sweatpants and a tee shirt pajamas) were stuck fast to his body with static cling, as was his wild mop of hair.

"What time is it?" Gabriel yawned.

"Time to get downstairs and help me with Grandpa," Mrs. Woods replied as she snagged a pair of Gabriel's blue jeans up off the floorboards and tossed them onto his bed. As the pants hit the comforter, a landslide of comic books poured out from under Gabriel's top sheet and spilled out all over the floor. Mrs. Woods stopped walking and rolled her eyes at her son. "Hurry up, I have breakfast waiting."

Gabriel and his mother lived in a run-down farmhouse just on the edge of the forest. It was an old house. Some said it was the oldest house left in Foxfield, and that was because it was the only original home left untouched by the ravenous forest. No one knows why, but for some strange reason the forest decided to give up and stop growing exactly one foot from the side of the house where a lone spruce tree blocked the back door to the kitchen. This, of course, made it nearly impossible to enter or exit the house through the back door; so Gabriel's mother simply left it unlocked.

Gabriel clambered down the old rotting staircase from his room in the attic and crashed himself down at the kitchen table.

Mrs. Woods was finishing her coffee while reading a two day old newspaper. "What's this?" Gabriel exclaimed as he spotted his plate.

"It's breakfast," Mrs. Woods replied dryly without lifting her eyes from the classifieds section. Gabriel looked at his breakfast. All he could see was a sliced up tomato and a spoon full of peanut butter.

"A tomato?" Gabriel glared at his food. "In the morning?"

"Sorry, kiddo. It's all we've got." Mrs. Woods stopped reading and shrugged. "Put some salt on the tomato. It's good. When I was a little girl we used to eat tomatoes like that all the time on hot summer days."

"It's September, mom. Summer was two months ago," Gabriel mumbled as he scooped up a glob of peanut butter and popped it into his mouth.

"Hurry up and finish eating so you can bring Grandpa his breakfast, and no screwing around. It's almost eight," Mrs. Woods replied as she looked back to the want ads.

"Aw, mom!" Gabriel stopped chewing and spoke through a mouth filled with sticky half-eaten peanut butter. "You know I hate crunchy peanut butter!"

Mrs. Woods stopped reading and lowered her paper. "Uh oh," she uttered.

"Uh oh?" Gabriel's face froze.

Mrs. Woods scrunched up her nose like she smelled something bad. "That's uh... not supposed to be crunchy."

Gabriel's grandfather, Grandpa Jerry lived out in the garage. At least they called it a garage. It was really more of a large wooden box loosely attached to the rest of the house by a few rusty nails and some spit.

After World War Two, Grandpa Jerry bought a new car and returned home to Foxfield. When he drove up in his fancy new car, he realized he didn't have a garage. So he did what came naturally, he built one. Decades later when Gabriel was born, Grandpa Jerry decided that the farmhouse was becoming too crowded and cramped for all four of them, so he decided to move out of the farmhouse and into the garage. There, Grandpa Jerry lived quietly with his two favorite possessions: his Studebaker and his old movie projector.

With a creak, Gabriel pushed open the large garage door while balancing a plate in his other hand.

"Morning Gabriel, where'ya been?" Grandpa Jerry asked as he sat comfortably in his pajamas and slippers behind the wheel of his Studebaker.

"Brushing my teeth," Gabriel groaned as he sat Grandpa Jerry's breakfast down on the seat next to him. Grandpa Jerry picked up the cup of coffee and glared down at the plate. "Market day, I take it?" he said with the raise of an old bushy eyebrow.

"Market day," Gabriel nodded. "And you may want to skip the peanut butter." Gabriel walked over to the bookshelf in the corner of the room and stared long and hard at the countless stacks of silver metal tins. "What will it be today, Grandpa?"

Grandpa raised a boney finger into the air. "The African Queen, if you please."

Gabriel's eyes quickly scanned the shelves. There were so many movie reels piled up on the dusty bookcase that it sometimes became difficult to read all the titles. "The Longest Day... Duck Soup... Vertigo... Ah, here we go!" Gabriel exclaimed as he tugged loose one of the tin canisters sandwiched between the bottom most stack. "Got it," he added as he removed the movie reel from within and threaded up the old projector in the back of the room. With a flick of the switch, the projector rattled to life and the garage was soon bathed in a beautiful silver light. Grandpa Jerry stared out the car's windshield and began nibbling on his tomato slices.

Gabriel stood and watched the movie for a moment or two to make sure everything was all right with the projector before he silently closed the garage door and pedaled off to school on his bike.

School, as always, was a drag, and Gabriel found most of the subjects to be pretty boring. Sometimes the history lessons could be cool when the teacher was talking about the Civil War or Custer's Last Stand, but usually the topic was something lame like fractions and Gabriel had a terrible time focusing. Instead, his attention would wander to the window and the corner of a small red brick building that lay just down the road.

This was how Gabriel spent the majority of his class time, staring out the window, straining his eyes to see the exact same corner of red brick day after day. It didn't matter how difficult it became. In the rain. In the snow. Even in the dead of winter when the windows would frost over completely, Gabriel would sit and stare vigilantly down the street at the building. However, all of this obsessive behavior was understandable because that red brick building happened to house Gabriel's absolute most favorite place on the face of the Earth, a comic book store known far and wide as Wonder Books.

Chapter Two:
WONDER BOOKS

At last, the final bell rang and Gabriel flew out the door like a shot. He scrambled his way through the sea of school children until he reached his trusty dirt bike. With a kick and a holler, he blasted off down the road, pedaling like wildfire until he reached his destination where he announced himself by locking his brakes and skidding to a stop in the gravel just outside the front door of Wonder Books.

Gabriel dropped his kickstand and threw open the door to the store. Immediately, he was overwhelmed by all of the wonderful sights and smells.

To Gabriel, nothing could compare to the smell of a comic book store. The fresh ink. The rubber molded toys. The smell of bubble gum from the baseball cards all lined up in a row behind the glass counter. Gabriel loved it all.

"Hello there, Gabe." Mr. Patrick, a silver haired old man in a black apron, greeted Gabriel as he entered the store. Gabriel nodded to the man as he strolled over to the tall wooden shelves filled to the brim with old comics. "What can I do for you today?"

"Just the usual," Gabriel replied as he hoisted a cardboard box full of loose comics off the shelf. He cradled the heavy box in his arms as he waddled like a penguin over to the corner. There, he dropped the box on the tile floor with a resounding thud. Kneeling beside the box, Gabriel removed the lid and began examining its contents carefully like an archeologist who just uncovered the artifacts of a lost civilization.

Then, just as he did every day after school, Gabriel removed each thin book one-by-one and carefully opened it under the warm glow of the old lamp in the corner. There he sat and examined every book in the box. Slowly he turned the pages, taking his time to read each line and absorb all the colors and imagery on every page. He often became lost somewhere within those pages, transforming himself into the Silver Bullet, Ironclad, or even the greatest superhero ever, The Eternal Guardian.

Eventually he would finish reading the comic book in hand and place it very carefully to one side of the box. He would stack and arrange each book by title and issue number always putting the oldest ones on the top. Every so often, he would take a break from reading and sit back against the exposed brick wall looking up at the numerous oak shelves that towered over his head. He often wondered what treasures he might find tucked away in the deepest corners of the topmost shelves. There were still hundreds of boxes on those shelves, and Gabriel planned on reading every comic in every box. That meant thousands upon thousands of possibilities for adventure, danger, heroics, and occasionally, romance (although he usually just skimmed those sorts of comic books).

Once he finished sorting through a particular box, he would return all the comics that he had examined with the exception of one or two that he carefully placed aside. Then he would mark the front of the box with the letters, G.W. (which were his initials of course), and gently return the box to its place on the shelf. Gathering up the comics he wished to keep, Gabriel walked up to the counter and layed them gently on the glass.

"Well, let's see here," Mr. Patrick looked over the top of his wire-rimmed spectacles at the two comics. One of them had a picture of a man riding a shark while fighting pirates, and the other had a hard-boiled detective on the cover wrestling with a man wearing a ski mask in a subway tunnel. "Oceanious, Warrior of Atlantis. Number seven and The Red Hammer number three. Oh my, well those are good ones aren't they?" Mr. Patrick smiled beneath his bristly white moustache. "That will be two dollars. Even." Gabriel reached into his pocket and removed two crumpled up dollar bills and placed them on the counter. Mr. Patrick scooped up the bills and opened the cash register. "You know, Gabriel, I should be paying you for organizing those old boxes for me," Mr. Patrick said as the cash register chimed.

"That's okay," Gabriel replied as he slid his new comics into a brown paper bag. "If you paid me for doing it, then it would just be work. Sort of like having an after school job and that would take some of the fun out of it, you know? I like things the way they are."

"That makes two of us." Mr. Patrick smiled as he handed two quarters back to Gabriel. "Frequent shopper discount," he added with a wink.

"Thanks." Gabriel took the coins and slid them into his pocket.

"Does your mother know you spend your lunch money on comic books?" Mr. Patrick asked with a raised eyebrow. Gabriel didn't answer. He just folded the top of the paper bag neatly with a sharp crease and turned towards the door. "Let me know when you want to get serious and talk about Riley," Mr. Patrick added in a curious tone of voice. Gabriel stopped walking; his hand was still on the doorknob.

Pausing for a moment, Gabriel turned back to the counter. "Sorry, Mr. Patrick. I told you before. He's not for sale."

"Are you sure about that Gabriel? I would take better care of him than anyone. In fact, he would go right up here on the wall of honor." Mr. Patrick gestured to the shelves behind the counter. There, on the topmost shelf, rested about a dozen different old comic books. Each one had a price tag next to it. The cheapest book on the shelf wore a tag of one thousand dollars. "Think about what you could do with that money! And of course I would let you come in and read it whenever you liked." Gabriel stared up at the shelf for a moment before snapping out of his trance.

Gabriel pushed open the door and smiled. "I'm sorry, Mr. Patrick, but Riley's not for sale. Not at any price."

Chapter Three:
AN UNEXPECTED VISITOR

The first few weeks of autumn were all alike. Gabriel would go to school, be bored, and spend the remainder of the afternoon sitting in Wonder Books sorting and reading old comics. To Gabriel life was pretty good. Or, at least it was consistent, which he figured was as good as it gets when you're twelve.

Every day, he would sit beneath the warm glow of the dusty antique lamp that rested in the corner of the store and lose himself within the thin colored pages of his favorite comics. He would sort out a box a day and leave with a few hand picked treasures tucked neatly under his arm. Then, one day, the unexpected happened.

Gabriel skidded his bike to a stop, just like he always did. Popped loose the kickstand, just like he always did. However, when he reached for the door, he found that his arm crumpled beneath his own weight causing him to plow face first into the thick glass that made up the comic book store's front door. Grabbing the metal handle with both hands, he pushed once again on the door. Then he pulled with all his might, but nothing happened. The door was locked! Shading his eyes with his hand, he leaned close to the glass and peered inside.

At first glance, everything seemed all right. The only thing out of place was that all of the lights were off, making the store, which always seemed warm and bright, suddenly feel very cold and empty to Gabriel.

He knocked on the glass and waited. No one answered.

Sticking his fingers through the mail slot, he held open the thin spring wound hatch and called out, "Hello?" He waited and tried again, but no one answered. Gabriel stepped back from the door and looked through the large glass window. He couldn't believe it, but it seemed that Wonder Books was closed.

Maybe Mr. Patrick was home sick today? Gabriel thought to himself as he got back on his bike and balanced himself upright with just the tips of his toes. Turning on his wheels, he pedaled down the street a few blocks then stopped. He looked back to the storefront that now seemed so very distant and cold. The store was still dark. "I suppose everyone gets sick once in a while," Gabriel muttered to himself and quickly bicycled home.

Time passed. Every day after school, Gabriel would hop on his bike and race like mad to Wonder Books, and every day the store was locked and dark. In the beginning, Gabriel would get off his bike and shake the locked door frantically, hoping it would magically spring open and Mr. Patrick would be waiting somewhere in the back room to turn on the lights and open the store. That, however, never happened. After a few days, Gabriel stopped getting off his bike altogether. He would just cruise past the comic book store and glance over in vain to see if there were any signs of life.

The store was always locked and dark.

None of this made any sense to Gabriel. What happened to Mr. Patrick? Why didn't he leave a note on the door, or at least put a closed sign in the window? Was he gone for good? Gabriel was beginning to wish he had taken Mr. Patrick's offer to work at the store. At least then he would have had a key and been able to get inside the shop. He was certain that if he were working for Mr. Patrick, then he would at least know what had happened to him. Gabriel thought all of this through as he rode past the store.

It was now late September, and Wonder Books had been closed for two weeks. Gabriel was beginning to worry if the store would ever open again. That's when he decided to look one last time into the shop and see if he could spot any sort of clue as to what had happened to Mr. Patrick. Coming to a slow stop, he parked his bike next to the front door (Gabriel never skidded to a stop anymore) and peered once more through the thick industrial glass.

Inside the store, it appeared as though everything was still there. The boxes were still on the shelves, the baseball cards were still in the case and the expensive, extremely rare comics were still resting on the topmost shelf right behind the counter. As far as Gabriel could tell, nothing was different. It was as if Mr. Patrick had been planning to come to work two weeks ago and simply never showed up.

Suddenly, Gabriel thought he saw something move within the store. It caught him off guard at first because he wasn't expecting to see anything at all. But then he saw it again; a flash of red. Something was creeping behind the thick wooden bookcases.

Pressing his face tight against the glass, he shaded his eyes with his hands and focused as hard as he could on the bookcase. What did he see? Gabriel rapped on the glass with his fist. The red something stopped moving. Gabriel could see a bit of it behind the bookcase, but he couldn't make out what it was. Was it an animal? Like a cat or dog? How did it get into the store when the building was locked up tight? Gabriel squinted into the dark room, fighting the image of his own reflection in the glass door.

He watched as the animal started to move again. Ever so slowly, the furry red creature peeked its reflective eyes out from behind the bookcase. Gabriel felt the hairs on the back of his neck bristle as the animal slowly turned its head and locked eyes with him. Gabriel could hardly breathe. The animal stepped out from behind the bookcase and started walking right toward the front door, its eyes still transfixed upon Gabriel. Gabriel felt his heart begin to race. Immediately, he recognized what type of creature it was, although he had never seen one face to face before. It was a fox.

The animal was bright red with black feet that made it look as if it were wearing little socks. As it walked, its large bushy white tail swung back and forth behind it in an almost hypnotic manner. The fox strolled halfway across the floor where it then sat down, never breaking eye contact with Gabriel.

Gabriel didn't dare breathe, and he wasn't certain what he should do. Time froze. The animal just sat there staring dead into Gabriel's eyes, never blinking, never moving. Suddenly the animal's eyes went wide and it hissed at Gabriel, baring a mouthful of sharp needle-like teeth. Even though there was an inch of thick glass between them, Gabriel leapt back.

"What's going on there?" A woman's voice called out somewhere behind Gabriel. Gabriel spun around to see a parking meter attendant glaring at him. "What are you doing there?" she asked again. Gabriel felt dumbfounded.

"There's... there's a fox in there," he said pointing to the front door of the comic book store.

"A fox? Ain't been no foxes 'round here for years," she replied as she walked up to the door of the bookstore. Gabriel stepped back as she looked through the glass. After a moment, she too cupped her hands to her eyes and looked through the glare. "No foxes in there. Maybe you saw a cat. Or a rat?" Gabriel quickly looked back into the store. The fox was gone.

"No. That was definitely a fox," he protested.

The meter maid shook her head and walked back over to her golf cart. "I'm telling ya kid, there ain't no foxes in Foxfield. Now don't be hanging around closed stores."

"Do you know? Is it closed for good?"

The meter maid looked up at the Wonder Books sign hanging over the store. "Sure looks like it to me," was all she said as she drove off down the street. Gabriel stood fixed to the spot. He looked back into the store one last time for any sign of the fox, but the meter maid was right. The fox had vanished.

Chapter Four:
THE SPECTACULAR OFFER

Gabriel raced home as fast as he could, pedaling his dirt bike with all his might. The sky seemed to be getting darker by the second. Charcoal gray storm clouds were rolling in and swiftly blotting out the blue sky. Gabriel wasn't too sure what time it was. He guessed it was about four o'clock in the afternoon, however it was getting so dark that it looked more like evening. Gabriel skidded his bike to a stop and raced into the farmhouse.

"Mom! Mom!" He called out as he opened the front door and flung his backpack onto the cluttered kitchen table. "Are you home?"

"Quit making such a racket," his mother called out from the next room. "I'm in here." Gabriel dashed over to the living room where his mother was sitting with a pile of clean laundry on her lap. She was folding and sorting the clothes into neat piles all around her chair. The television was on, but the volume was so low that Gabriel could barely hear it. "Keep it down will you? Grandpa's napping." Mrs. Woods gestured with her head to the left while she rolled a pair of socks into a tight springy ball. Gabriel looked over to see Grandpa Jerry passed out on the couch.

"You are never going to believe what I just saw!" Gabriel exclaimed as he plopped himself down in the tattered armchair.

"News says that a big storm's blowing in." Mrs. Woods commented as she folded one of Gabriel's old tees and rested it on top of a stack of worn out shirts. "I don't know how you manage to keep getting these clothes so dirty. You spend all of your free time at that bookstore. You never go out for sports. I just don't get it."

"Mom. I'm trying to tell you something really cool here," Gabriel exasperated.

"Yeah? What is it?"

"I saw something today. Something amazing!" Gabriel continued.

DING-DONG!

Mrs. Woods sat up in her chair spilling a stack of neatly folded dungarees on the floor. "Someone's at the door?"

"Mom!"

"Hang on a second. You can tell me your really cool thing in a minute." Mrs. Woods sighed as she got up and walked out of the living room. Gabriel slumped in his easy chair. Staring at the TV, he saw the weather report showing a giant storm moving in over all of Massachusetts. Warnings were flashing across the bottom of the screen, something about a nor'easter. "Gabriel. Someone's here to see you." Mrs. Woods called out from the other room.

"For me? Who is it?" Gabriel yelled back. But his mother didn't answer. Pulling himself up from his chair, Gabriel dragged himself to the front door.

Standing outside on the porch was the smallest man Gabriel had ever seen. He wore a brown striped suit and in his right hand he carried a black leather briefcase. The tiny man had a bit of a hooked nose that whistled as he spoke. "Hello there? Master Gabriel Woods I presume?" the man asked.

"Master?" Gabriel raised an eyebrow to his mother.

"It means young man," Mrs. Woods shrugged.

"Ahem, yes." The short man continued, "I've come a long way to make you quite a spectacular offer."

"Okay," Gabriel slowly replied. "What is it?"

"It has come to my attention that you are in possession of an extremely rare comic book." Gabriel's eyes began to glaze over as the man spoke, as if he had heard this speech a million times before. "A comic that I have scoured the globe searching for but have never been able to find, until now." Gabriel looked up to his mother who also seemed to know what was coming next. "Yes, Master Gabriel. You are in possession of the first issue of the classic wartime comic, Riley: Ace of the Skies. An extremely rare comic that was only printed for a short while during World War Two."

"What makes you think that I have it?" Gabriel asked as he leaned against the doorframe.

"A Mr. Patrick at that Wonder Bookstore answered my advertisement. He told me that you were in possession of such a comic and that you might be interested in selling it for, how shall I say, the right price."

"Mr. Patrick! When did you see him?" Gabriel interjected. The little man appeared surprised by Gabriel's outburst, and he fumbled for a moment with his briefcase.

"I have never met Mr. Patrick face to face, I'm sorry to say. I was hoping to speak with him this afternoon, but unfortunately his store was closed when I arrived."

"Oh." Gabriel's face dropped. "Well, I'm sorry you've come so far, but it's not for sale."

All of the color suddenly drained from the stranger's face. "You mean to say you do have it. Here in this, um, house?" The little man's eyes grew wide as he attempted to peek through the door into the kitchen. "Is there any chance I may see it, please?"

"Sorry, Mr..." Gabriel stumbled on his words realizing he didn't even know this man's name.

"Higby." The little man quickly finished Gabriel's sentence. "Mr. Higby."

"Sorry, Mr. Higby, but I'm not selling that comic book, ever." Gabriel finished his statement.

"That comic means a lot to him." Mrs. Woods added, placing her hand on Gabriel's shoulder. "You're not the first person that's come around here looking. A lot of people have tried offering him money for it."

"Sorry, but it's not for sale." Gabriel smiled a weak smile.

"I'll pay you ten thousand dollars for it." Mr. Higby said coolly. Gabriel didn't even blink.

"No sale."

"Twenty five thousand dollars." Mr. Higby swiftly interjected, almost overlapping Gabriel's words. Gabriel could feel his mother's hand squeezing his shoulder tighter. "Thirty thousand dollars. That's my final offer." Mr. Higby said proudly. Gabriel winced as he felt his mother's vice-like grip dig deep into his shoulder.

Gabriel looked into Mr. Higby's eyes for a moment then simply said, "No thank you. Goodbye, Mr. Higby," and began to close the front door.

"Wait! Here!" Mr. Higby forced his arm though the gap, jamming it tight between the door and the frame. In his fingers was a small white card. Mrs. Woods plucked the card from his hand and read it aloud.

WILLIAM HIGBY
INVESTMENT COLLECTIBLES
NEW YORK, LONDON, TOKYO
555-314-2299

"Call me day or night when you're ready to sell, lad. I can be up here in less than five hours. Cash in hand!" Gabriel heard Mr. Higby's words through the door as his mother shoved the man's arm back and closed the door tightly behind it.

"Well, he was an energetic little spud," Mrs. Woods commented as she handed Gabriel the business card. "I guess you can put that one with the others." Gabriel glanced at the card and shoved it into the pocket of his jeans as the two walked back out to the living room. "You know, you really should consider selling that old book one of these days. I mean that was a lot of money he was offering us. That could be your college fund, you know." Returning to her chair Mrs. Woods picked up her laundry and continued folding. "So what was that really cool thing you wanted to tell me?"

Chapter Five:
THE COMING STORM

Gabriel flopped back down in his easy chair and propped his legs up. "Oh, it was nothing."

"Nothing, eh? It didn't seem like nothing when you came in the door," Mrs. Woods replied in a sly tone of voice, her eyes never leaving her folding. Gabriel peeked out of the corner of his eye to see if his mother was really interested, but she just continued sorting socks and paying him no mind.

"No. No. I don't think you would find it very cool at all." Gabriel drawled as he pulled Mr. Higby's business card from his back pocket and pretended to examine it.

"Okay then. Don't tell me." Mrs. Woods calmly replied. "Instead, why don't you tell me what you learned in school today?"

"It was a fox." Gabriel quickly snapped.

"You learned about foxes in school?"

"No. I saw a fox. A real live one. Here in town."

Gabriel's mother finally stopped folding clothes and slowly looked over at Gabriel. "There aren't any foxes in Foxfield," she finally said shaking her head.

"Well there are now," Gabriel replied. "At least there's one."

"A fox? Are you sure it wasn't just a cat with a bushy tail? Or a raccoon? Where did you see it?" Mrs. Woods asked.

"It was in the comic book store," Gabriel answered.

"I thought you told me the comic book store was closed?"

"It is closed, but I was looking through the glass door and there it was. Walking around the store."

No one spoke. The sky was becoming dark as pitch and they sat and listened to the sound of raindrops rapping against the window.

After a moment, Gabriel's mother finally broke the silence. "I don't want you going near that thing if you see it again. All right?" Her tone of voice seemed grim to Gabriel and he felt like there was something she wasn't telling him. "In fact, if you even see that fox again I want you to call me right away. Do you promise?"

Gabriel thought his mother seemed to be over-reacting a bit, but in the end he conceded. "I promise."

"Listen to your mother, Gabriel," an old tired voice suddenly rose up from the couch. Gabriel looked over to see Grandpa Jerry staring at him from beneath a pile of afghans. "She knows what she's talking about." Grandpa Jerry spoke as he pulled himself up from the mountain of covers and propped himself awkwardly on the edge of the sofa. "Foxes are nothing but trouble." Gabriel cracked a broad grin. "What are you smiling about son? This isn't a laughing matter." Gabriel found it difficult to take his grandfather seriously when he had a freshly washed sock stuck to the side of his head with static cling. Mrs. Woods reached over and peeled the sock off. "Thank you, my dear," Grandpa Jerry nodded to Mrs. Woods before turning his attention back to Gabriel. "You listen to me. I know what I'm talking about."

The rain was really coming down now, and it sounded more like someone was dumping a barrel of nails on the roof than raindrops. "They're just dumb animals." Gabriel shrugged.

"Nothing dumb about those animals son. They're smart. A lot smarter than you and I could possibly imagine, and devious. You know it when a fox is working out an angle on you." Grandpa Jerry pointed two fingers at Gabriel's eyes as he spoke. "They just sit there, staring right through you like you weren't even there." Gabriel shook off a small chill that danced down his spine.

"Once they figure you out, that's when they go to work on you."

"Go to work?"

"Knock it off, Dad," Mrs. Woods chimed in. "You're not helping."

"It's true," Grandpa Jerry added ignoring Gabriel's mother. "Foxes are actually servants of the Devil. They help him do his dirty work. It's a bad omen when they come to town. It means something bad is about to happen. Real bad. They're worse than black cats, they are."

"Then how come there have never been any foxes in Foxfield?" Gabriel looked over at his mother. "Until now, I mean."

"There used to be foxes here, thick as weeds, but then the forest grew. Nature expelled them like man being expelled from the garden of Eden. That's why we're protected from evil here. That's why this little town is so quiet and safe. There's something in the forest. Something that keeps danger at bay."

"Don't be ridiculous, Dad," Mrs. Woods replied. "If that's true, why haven't I heard this story before?"

Grandpa Jerry shrugged and cocked an eyebrow at Mrs. Woods. "You've never asked."

With a brilliant flash of white light, the television suddenly erupted with noise and static before blinking off. All of the rest of the lights and appliances did the same. Gabriel, Mrs. Woods and Grandpa Jerry were all suddenly plunged into complete and utter darkness. The only sound they could hear was that of the rain pounding wildly against the windows and the distant echo of thunder.

"Oh great, the power's out," Mrs. Woods groaned. "Darn storm."

Chapter Six:
RILEY: ACE OF THE SKIES

Gabriel sat on his bed. It was nearly ten o'clock at night, and the storm continued to rage outside his bedroom window. The power was still out and the only source of light came from the small paraffin wax lantern resting on the end table next to his headboard. Gabriel stared out the window and listened to the storm winds howl and the thunder crash. A river of water was rushing down the windowpane distorting Gabriel's reflection. Every so often the lightning would flash, flaring up ghostly outlines of the nearby forest. Gabriel wondered if the rain would ever stop.

"Still awake?" Mrs. Woods asked as she peeked through the crack in the doorway.

"Yeah. Sort of," Gabriel replied as he adjusted his pajamas.

"It's really coming down now, isn't it?" Mrs. Woods walked into the room and sat at the foot of Gabriel's bed.

"Yeah. I guess so," Gabriel replied in a whisper, his eyes transfixed on the hypnotic patterns rolling down his window. Mrs. Woods looked over and she too was soon hypnotized by the rain. "You think school will be closed tomorrow?" Gabriel asked.

"I wouldn't get my hopes up, kiddo. We've seen a lot worse weather than this," she replied. Again the lightning flashed. For an instant, Gabriel could make out the billowing treetops. "Gabriel, can I talk to you about something important?" Mrs. Woods asked.

"Sure. What is it?" Gabriel replied.

"I think you should seriously consider selling that old comic book of yours."

Gabriel snapped out of his trance and looked wide eyed at his mother. "What!"

"I think it's time you sold that old comic book. Many different people have come here over the years offering you a lot of money for it. I think it's time you picked an offer and sold it." Mrs. Woods spoke with authority but also with a hint of pain in her voice.

Gabriel sighed to himself and moaned, "Aw, Mom. Why should I do that? I don't want to sell it off to some stranger. It's my comic. I don't want to sell it."

"Look around you, Gabriel." Mrs. Woods gestured to numerous cardboard boxes and bookshelves surrounding Gabriel's room, all of which were overflowing with comics. "You have tons of comic books. More than you can ever really read. Why can't you sell just this one? That money could be your college fund, and you know it would be a big help with your father gone now." Mrs. Woods suddenly fell silent, and she covered her mouth with her hand. Gabriel's face dropped, and he looked down at his lap. "I'm sorry, honey." Mrs. Woods cried. "I didn't mean to say that. I know you miss your dad." Gabriel said nothing. He simply stared at his feet. The room fell cold and silent. The winds outside continued to blow and howl. For an instant, Gabriel felt the bitter wind run across his floor and up over his bed. Even the magic of the stormy windowpane seemed to lose all of its seduction and charm. "Honey. I'm sorry. Listen, you don't have to sell that comic book if you don't want to."

A long silence filled the room as the warm firelight of the lantern danced across the walls. Mrs. Woods waited a moment before getting up and walking back over to the door.

"I can't sell that comic book, Mom," Gabriel finally answered. "It's the only thing I have left that reminds me of him. Reminds me of Dad."

Gabriel's mother smiled softly to herself. "Then you hold on to it and someday, if you want to, you can sell it when you're good and ready. Now, lights out. There might be school tomorrow." And with that, she kissed Gabriel on the forehead and closed the door tight.

Gabriel leaned over and turned the small metal knob that lowered the wick back into the lantern. Slowly but surely, the room grew dark.

Gabriel lay in the darkness and listened to the rain pounding down on the roof. His bedroom was actually part of the attic so the din of the storm really resonated around his bedchamber. Again the lightning flashed, but this time Gabriel noticed how it seemed to light up his walls more than the trees outside.

"Dad," he whispered. He slid off his mattress and knelt down on the floor. Reaching under his bed Gabriel pulled out a weathered and dented old shoebox. He removed the lid and reached into the box. He then pulled out a cylindrical object wrapped up tight in an old plastic grocery bag. With the precision of a surgeon, he slid off the protective bag and gently removed the object within. It was a very old and very worn comic book.

The cover of the comic had a man with a well-chiseled jaw wearing a brown leather jacket and a large billowing white scarf flowing in the breeze behind him. In his right hand, he held an enormous American flag and in his left, he held the torn remains of a Nazi banner. Behind this pilot was the most glorious looking fighter plane Gabriel had ever seen, and across the top of the cover, the words RILEY: ACE OF THE SKIES were printed in bold daring type. This comic book was Gabriel's prize possession, and he held it ever so gently in his hands as he examined it.

Gabriel climbed back up and propped the comic on his nightstand so he could look at it as he lay in bed. Rolling over onto his back, he stared out the window once more. The lightning flashed, and suddenly, all of the color vanished from Gabriel's cheeks. His eyes grew wide, and the palms of his hands became clammy and cold. Staring at him from outside the window was the fox.

It sat perched on the thin ledge of the windowsill. The rain raced down the fox's body and splashed wildly around its feet. The animal's fur was matted and soaked. When the wind flared up, it sent a blast through the creature's coat that whipped its tail into a frenzy. The fox was staring directly at Gabriel. Its jaw was quivering from the cold.

Gabriel felt his throat run dry. He wanted to call for his mother, but when he tried to yell, all that came out was a weak cough. The fox just sat there in the downpour locking eyes with Gabriel. Never blinking. Never moving.

Fumbling in the dark, Gabriel felt around on the end table for his lantern. Finding it, he reached out for the book of matches his mother had given him and struck a match.

For an instant, the fox's eyes darted to the lit match then back to Gabriel. Gabriel kept his eyes on the fox as he felt in the darkness for the lantern's cloth wick and lit it. The room began to glow in the warm firelight. Gabriel raised the lantern up to the window and looked for the fox, but now (because of the bright lantern light) all he could see was his own reflection looking back at him in the glass.

This was worse. Now he couldn't see the fox at all and Gabriel's imagination ran wild. He imagined the fox slipping into his bedroom when he wasn't looking, scurrying across the floor and tucking itself into a dark corner. There the fox would hide and wait for the opportunity to kill Gabriel in his sleep. With a twist of the knob, Gabriel extinguished the lantern. In an instant his own reflection vanished from the window. Unfortunately, so had the fox.

C h a p t e r   S e v e n :
OCTOBER FIRST

It had been a very long night. Gabriel was relieved when the storm finally died out and the sun slowly crept up over the treetops. He had spent the entire night sitting up in his bed with his football helmet on and his Louisville slugger resting across his lap. It was seven o'clock in the morning when his mother opened his bedroom door and sang, "Rise and shine... oh my. Gabriel?"

Gabriel fought to open a weighty eyelid and peek out at his mother. "Mom? Is that you?" His football helmet was slumped awkwardly across his brow and he could only see out of one side.

"What the heck are you doing?" Mrs. Woods asked as she walked over to the window and forced it open with a bang. Cool crisp autumn air rushed in. The brisk air felt good, and Gabriel thought, just for a moment, that he could smell the ocean.

"That fox came back last night," Gabriel mumbled as he flopped down against his propped up pillows. His old wooden bat hit the floor with a bang and a rattle. "He was over there." Gabriel hoisted a tired arm and pointed at the window.

"Out the window?" Mrs. Woods asked. Gabriel's head nodded yes like an old rag doll. Sticking her head out the window, Mrs. Woods examined the sharp slope of the roof. "It was out here? During the storm?" Again Gabriel flopped his head yes. "Uh-huh." Mrs. Woods grunted. "Are you sure you didn't just have a nightmare?" Gabriel was now stretched across the bed with his football helmet head hanging off the far side.

"It wasn't a dream." He yawned.

"Okay, it wasn't a dream, but real or not, you need to get ready for school and I need to get ready for work."

"Can't I stay home today? I'm so tired." Gabriel protested. Mrs. Woods walked over and twisted the football helmet off his head.

"Do you really want to stay here alone with all these foxes running around?"

"I think it was the same fox from yesterday." Gabriel rubbed the sleep from his eyes.

"And what makes you say that?" Mrs. Woods returned Gabriel's helmet to the closet shelf.

"It was the way he was staring at me."

Gabriel argued with his mother over staying home for another twenty minutes and in the end, as always, his mother prevailed. Patting him on the head, Mrs. Woods kissed Gabriel on his cheek and sent him off down the road to school on his dirt bike.

Foxfield was a mess. Everywhere Gabriel looked trees lay toppled, branches were broken, and he could barely pedal his bike due to the deep puddles and slippery wet leaves that were caked all over the pavement. As he rode to school, he even saw a few toppled telephone poles and a thick black electrical cable that was slithering its way across the pavement, throwing off hot sparks as it went.

Washington Irving Elementary School wasn't in much better shape. The power was still out, and the buses were unable to get into the parking lot due to the large oak tree that had fallen across the driveway. However, even with all those setbacks the school day started as usual. Gabriel sat in his class-room, slumped across his desk, looking out the window as he always did.

Out in the distance, he could see the familiar red brick corner of the comic book store. Suddenly, a horrifying thought crossed his mind. Wonder Books! Was it alright? If the storm did this much damage to the town, he could only imagine the state of the comic shop. Maybe a tree limb got caught up in the powerful winds and smashed through the glass front of the store. Then the storm would blow open all of the boxes, scattering the comics thorough the streets like someone flinging a pack of cards into the wind. On top of that, the rain would most certainly ruin all the pages of each book. The inks would become blotted and the delicate paper would be ripped apart. The entire town square would be plastered with the shredded remains of his favorite comic books. Once the damage was done, the rains would come pouring through the gaping hole in the glass and the store would most certainly flood. Nothing would be left! This was a real emergency! Without warning, Gabriel stood up in his seat, and strained to see if he could spy the extent of the damage from here.

"Mr. Woods? Is there something wrong?" Gabriel's teacher, Mr. Silverman, was staring at him from the front of the classroom. He had a rather puzzled look on his face. Gabriel felt himself blush. "What is it, Gabriel?" he asked as he tapped his finger loudly against the blackboard. Gabriel didn't know what to say, as his eyes darted around the class from face to face. Everyone was looking at him wondering what was wrong.

"I... uh," Gabriel stammered, "I need to go."

"Go?" Mr. Silverman shook his head at Gabriel. "To the bathroom?"

"Yeah." Gabriel nodded and began faking the pee-pee dance. "That's it. I need to go the bathroom real bad." Mr. Silverman rolled his eyes and walked over to his desk where he removed a worn down wooden block with the words HALL-PASS scribbled across it in thick black magic marker.

"We're about to discuss the Northwest Expansion, and this will be on the test." Mr. Silverman explained as he handed Gabriel the wooden block. "So be quick."

"Got it. Northwest Expansion. I'll be right back. Thanks," Gabriel sputtered as he dashed out the door.

The hallway appeared to be deserted. Gabriel moved swiftly through the school. He silently slipped through the building until he was able to make his way outside to the bike rack. Gabriel unlocked his bike and glanced around to make sure no one was watching. The coast looked clear, so he rode off towards Wonder Books as quickly as he could.

The town square was also in complete ruin. Gabriel felt his stomach churn as he passed the pharmacy. Its windows were destroyed and several shelves were knocked over. Gabriel began to pedal harder. The ice cream shop was also pretty battered. As he passed by, Gabriel could see Mr. Martelli inside using garbage cans to collect the rainwater that was dripping from the ceiling. Almost there. Gabriel rode past the church and the library and now he could see the red brick side of Wonder Books. Glancing at the town clock, he saw that he had already been gone for seven minutes. He wondered how long he had until Mr. Silverman would start getting suspicious. Skidding to a stop, Gabriel's jaw dropped open as he spied the front of the comic book store.

At first glance, it appeared there was nothing wrong with Wonder Books. There was no damage anywhere to the face of the building. The glass windows were still intact. The front door was fine. It was as if the storm had passed through the town and missed the comic book store altogether.

However, that wasn't the reason Gabriel's mouth had fallen open. His mouth was gaping like a fish because the entire inside of Wonder Books was now completely and utterly empty. Nothing remained. The large wooden bookcases were gone. The lamp in the corner was gone. The glass case up front was gone. Even the incredibly rare comics up on the highest shelf were now missing as was the shelf itself. But most importantly of all, every single comic book in the store was gone. Nothing remained. The entire store had been cleared out during the night.

Gabriel couldn't believe what he saw. He pressed his face right up against the glass and shaded his eyes with his hand. All he could see was one large empty room. All that remained were the floor tiles and a few bits of wire dangling down where some cardboard displays used to hang. Then Gabriel spotted something even stranger.

There was a light on in the back room of the shop, and a warm orange glow filled the doorway. Was Mr. Patrick back? Was that the light of the lamp that used to be in the corner? Gabriel knocked hard on the glass. The light began to flicker in a strange way. Gabriel knocked again. For an instant, he saw the shadow of a man moving within the light. He knocked harder this time in hopes of getting the man's attention. His mind was racing with questions. What happened to the comic books? Was that Mr. Patrick? Why did this building have power when no one else in town did?

"Mr. Patrick!" Gabriel shouted through the glass as he pounded the palm of his hand against the door. The shadow stopped moving. Maybe he heard him? "Mr. Patrick!" he bellowed.

"Hey, you there!" Gabriel looked over his shoulder to see the same meter maid from yesterday standing on the corner. "You again?" Her hands were on her hips, and she looked upset. "What did I tell you about hanging around closed shops! And why aren't you in school?"

Chapter Eight:
DOUBLE TROUBLE

"And that's where I found him." The meter maid had just finished telling her story to Mr. Silverman and Principal Watts. Gabriel stood silently; his head bowed looking at his shoes.

Principal Watts cleared his throat. "Ahem, well thank you, Mrs..."

"Miss Marshal," the meter maid said with a smile as she tapped the plastic nametag pinned to her uniform.

"Miss Marshal. Yes, thank you for bringing Gabriel back to us."

"It was no problem. I would keep an eye on him though. That's the second time I've caught him loitering around that comic book store."

"We'll notify his parents. Thank you again," Principal Watts replied as he shook her hand and walked Miss Marshal out of his office. Mr. Silverman stood in front of Gabriel with his arms crossed. They were all alone in the principal's office.

"What were you thinking, Gabriel?" Mr. Silverman sighed. "You abused my trust and did something really stupid. You're lucky nothing happened to you. You're my responsibility while you're in my class. You know that? What came over you?"

At first, Gabriel didn't say anything. He just kept looking down at his feet, occasionally flicking his untied shoelace with his toe. "I'm sorry, Mr. Silverman," was all he eventually muttered.

"Well, you should be, Gabriel," Mr. Silverman grunted. "Geesh. We're both going to be in trouble now."

The door opened and closed with a bang. Principal Watts walked calmly to his desk and sat down in his chair. He pulled out a ballpoint pen and wrote a few lines on his personal letterhead. When he had finished, he placed the letter in an envelope and sealed it.

"Have a seat, Gabriel." Principal Watts gestured to the blue plastic chair in front of his desk. Gabriel sat down. "You know that students aren't allowed to leave the campus during school hours, correct?" Gabriel was still silent. "Correct?" Principal Watts reiterated louder and with more gusto.

"Yes," Gabriel mumbled.

"Pardon me?" Principal Watts exclaimed leaning his ear toward Gabriel.

"Correct, Principal Watts," Gabriel said in a clear but nervous voice.

"Good. I'm glad you understand the rules, Gabriel." Principal Watts then picked up the sealed envelope and held it out for Gabriel to take. "I want you to bring this letter home, and give it to your father and mother. I want it signed by both parents and returned to me before class starts tomorrow morning. Do you understand me?"

"Yes, sir," Gabriel replied as he took the envelope from Principal Watts' outstretched hand.

"Very good." Principal Watts nodded. "On top of which, you will have detention with Mr. Silverman every Wednesday after school from now until holiday break in December." Gabriel grimaced upon hearing his sentence and looked over to Mr. Silverman who was simply shaking his head at Gabriel with a stern look on his face. "That will be all, Mr. Woods. I want you to return to your classroom, and wait at your desk until the late bell rings. Then you may go home." Principal Watts dismissed Gabriel with a wave of his hand.

Gabriel walked over to the door and stopped. "Principal Watts."

"Yes, Gabriel."

"I don't think I can have my father sign this note," Gabriel said holding up the sealed envelope.

"And why is that?" Principal Watts folded his hands on his desk and glared at Gabriel.

"Because he's dead," Gabriel replied flatly.

Principal Watts' expression seemed to fall from his face leaving only a blank self-conscious stare. "Then your mother's signature will suffice."

"All right," Gabriel said as he headed for the door.

"Come on Gabriel, I'll walk you back to class." Mr. Silverman patted Gabriel on the shoulder as he opened the principal's door.

"Hang on a minute, Mr. Silverman. I think I need to have a word with you as well. You may go back alone, Gabriel. Ask the secretary for a hall pass on the way out."

Gabriel turned and exited the office. Looking back, he could see Mr. Silverman frowning, giving Gabriel the sort of look that you knew meant, "Just look at the mess you've gotten me into."

Chapter Nine:
A PART OF THE SOLUTION

"You did what?" Mrs. Woods clutched Gabriel's note so tightly in her right hand that it became bent and crumpled.

"I never meant to be gone that long," Gabriel argued.

"That's besides the point, Gabriel. You did something very dumb and dangerous today. There were power lines down all over town. That big tree fell across Main Street. There's broken glass everywhere. What if something had happened to you? No one would have known where you were." Mrs. Woods sat down at the kitchen table across from Gabriel and looked at his note again. "Oh, Gabe," she finally sighed in defeat.

"I'm sorry, mom," Gabriel squeaked meekly.

"I just need to be able to trust you, Gabriel," Mrs. Woods confided. "Especially with your dad gone. It's tough enough for me taking care of all three of us without needing to worry about what you're doing, too." Placing the note on the kitchen table, Mrs. Woods ironed out the wrinkles with the palm of her hand, smoothing the paper over and over again, until it lay flat. "Hand me that pen will you?" Gabriel reached over and gave his mother the old ballpoint pen resting on the counter next to a To-Do list from six months ago. Taking the pen in hand, Mrs. Woods worked the tip of it on a scrap of paper until the ink began to flow. Then she signed her name at the bottom and dated it. "Here you go." Mrs. Woods held out the note. Gabriel tried to take the paper from his mother's hand but found that she held onto it with an iron grip. "Listen to me carefully, Gabriel," Mrs. Woods began to speak, staring dead into Gabriel's eyes. "You're off the hook with me this time. But I want you to promise me, no more foolishness. I need you to be the man of the house. I need you to step up and help be part of the solution, not a part of the problem. I'm depending on you. Who knows, someday something may happen to me, and I need to know you will be there to help. Got it?"

Gabriel didn't know what to say. He wanted to speak, but his throat felt dry and scratchy. "I promise, Mom," was all he was able to muster. Mrs. Woods' grip loosened as the note slipped from her hand into Gabriel's.

"Good." Mrs. Woods smiled as she picked up her green apron and car keys. "You can start being part of the solution tonight by helping with the dishes."

"Aw, mom..." Gabriel groaned, but Mrs. Woods flashed him such a stern glare that his mouth snapped shut causing his teeth to click together.

"Very good." Mrs. Woods smiled. "I need to work the night shift tonight, so I want you to be in bed by nine thirty, understand?"

"Sure thing," Gabriel nodded.

Mrs. Woods opened the front door, then stopped with a lurch as if she suddenly remembered something. "Oh Gabriel, I want you to keep your bedroom window closed from now on."

"My window?" Gabriel asked.

"Yeah. Your window. In fact, try and keep all the windows in the house closed from now on, and locked too."

"Why is that, mom?"

Mrs. Woods glanced over to the edge of the forest that was being illuminated by the last rays of the setting sun. "It's because you're not the only one who's seen foxes around here. Apparently, the town seems to be overrun with them. It was in the paper today. They appear to be everywhere."

"Does anyone know where they came from?" Gabriel asked.

Mrs. Woods shook her head. "They're not sure, but some people think the storm must have flushed them out of the forest."

Chapter Ten:
A SURPRISE NOTE

The next morning Gabriel awoke not to the sounds of his mother's voice, but to the discovery that a piece of loose-leaf paper had been scotch-taped to his forehead sometime in the night. Gabriel sat up in bed and peeled the tape off his brow. There was a message on the paper that read:

> Gabriel,
>
> Had to work late last night, so I'm sleeping in
> this morning. Be sure to take care of Grandpa Jerry
> before you go to school. Lunch is in the fridge.
>
> Love, Mom

Gabriel climbed out of bed and got himself ready for school without a hitch. Opening the garage door, he found Grandpa Jerry already resting in the front seat of his Studebaker waiting for the movie to start.

"You're late." He coughed.

"Mom didn't wake me up. She had to work late," Gabriel replied as he pulled a film tin off the shelf and brushed the dust from the lid with his arm. Spooling up the projector, he flicked off the lights and closed the garage door to the sound of the MGM lion roaring loudly.

Arriving at school, Gabriel headed directly to the front office. "Principal Watts is very busy right now, but you can leave him a note," the secretary said to Gabriel as she blocked the door to the principal's office.

"He wanted me to give him this," Gabriel replied, holding out the note his mother had signed the night before.

The secretary took the wrinkled letter from Gabriel's hand and examined it as if it was some type of disgusting insect. "I'll give this to Principal

Watts as soon as he finishes his meeting," she replied as she dumped the sorry looking scrap of paper onto her desk.

The rest of the day seemed to progress without incident. Gabriel tried to keep his attention on Mr. Silverman's lectures and not on the familiar red brick building resting out the window. However Gabriel couldn't keep his mind from wandering.

Who was that in the comic book store yesterday? What happened to all the comics? How could someone possibly empty out the entire comic book store in one night, especially with a storm like that tearing apart the whole town? Gabriel's mind was racing with questions and he needed to get some answers.

"Alright class. If you will please open your English books to page seventy-seven, we will continue reading Johnny Tremain aloud. Michael, please pick up where we left off yesterday." Mr. Silverman motioned to the fat boy in the red sweater who sat in the front row of the classroom.

Gabriel reached into his backpack and removed his tattered English book. Turning the pages, Gabriel eventually came to page seventy-seven and found the place where his classmate was reading aloud. However, there appeared to be something wrong with his textbook. In the middle of his book was a strange lump that Gabriel hadn't noticed before. It looked like something was wedged deep in the center of his textbook, making the pages bulge out right around the spine. Gabriel flipped the pages quickly with his thumb until he came to the strange lump.

There in the center of his book was what appeared to be an object wrapped in large green oak leaves and tied together like a small bundle with long slender blades of grass. Picking up the tiny bundle Gabriel carefully untied the delicate grass strings and unwrapped the strange little package on the pages of his textbook. The leaves quickly unraveled themselves as a handful of rich dark soil poured out all over Gabriel's desk.

Was this someone's idea of a practical joke? Gabriel thought to himself as he rubbed the black grit from his fingertips. Looking down he was about to brush the dirt off his desk when he suddenly noticed something both strange and amazing!

The soil that had poured out onto his desk appeared to form words. At first, he thought his eyes were playing tricks on him. Maybe he was too tired from all the strange events over the past few days, but there it was in plain English. The dirt spelled out a message. Three simple words.

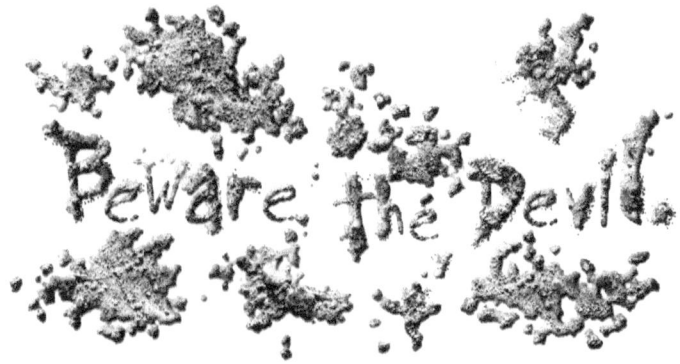

"Beware?" Gabriel said aloud to himself.

"Excuse me?" Mr. Silverman glanced up from his extra fat teacher's edition. "Did you say something, Gabriel?"

"What?" Gabriel's head darted back and forth across the classroom. Everywhere he looked students were staring back at him with curious blank eyes.

"Are you alright, Gabriel? You don't look so good, and you're all sweaty." Mr. Silverman stood up from his desk and started walking towards Gabriel. With a sweep of his arm, Gabriel brushed the dirt across his desk smearing the soil until the words were unintelligible. "What happened to your desk?" Mr. Silverman ran his finger through the dark grit covering Gabriel's desktop. "It's filthy."

"Sorry about that. I guess I dropped my book on the way home from school the other day. It fell in the dirt." Gabriel knew his excuse was pretty thin, but he had to tell Mr. Silverman something.

"And your sleeve? I suppose you dropped that in the dirt as well?" Mr. Silverman tugged at the arm Gabriel used to sweep off the desk. It too was covered in soil. Gabriel didn't have an answer for that. He stammered for a moment, then simply shrugged. "You've been acting very strange lately, Gabriel." Mr. Silverman peered down his nose at Gabriel.

"You're telling me," Gabriel replied with a nervous looking smile. Mr. Silverman did not return the smile. He simply turned and walked back to his desk where he asked the students to continue reading aloud.

Gabriel pretended to read along, but his eyes never seemed to find the page. His mind began to race as he rubbed the dirt back and forth between his finger and his thumb. He needed to go back to the comic book store. He needed to find out who that was he saw in the backroom. What happened to all the comic books? How on Earth did someone clear out an entire store in one stormy night? And now, who sent him that message in the dirt?

It was then and there that Gabriel decided no matter what, today would be the day he would start getting some answers. And he would start at the source of it all, Wonder Books.

Chapter Eleven:
WICKED BOOKS

Eventually the final bell rang and school was dismissed. Gabriel raced through the hallways as fast as he could until he reached his bike and sped off down the street towards the comic book store.

Arriving at the store, Gabriel's eyes grew wide as he slowed his bike to a gradual stop in front of the shop's brick façade. At first he couldn't believe his eyes. The lights inside the store were all on and a new looking white and blue OPEN sign now rested on the dusty metal window ledge.

This was amazing! It appeared as if the store was indeed open again. It had been almost a month since Mr. Patrick had first vanished, and as he approached the front door, Gabriel could see the unmistakable sight of someone sitting at the counter reading a newspaper. Gabriel couldn't tell if it was Mr. Patrick or not. The man held the paper upright blocking any view of his face.

Gripping the metal handle with his hands, Gabriel took a deep breath and pulled.

Clang!

The deadbolt banged loudly against the doorframe. "What!" Gabriel exclaimed as he tugged on the door again. He yanked on the handle rattling the door back and forth. The door was definitely locked tight. Gabriel rapped on the glass in an attempt to get the attention of the man behind the counter. "Hello?" Gabriel called out through the glass. "Hello, Mr. Patrick?"

The mystery man behind the counter didn't flinch. He simply continued reading his paper, occasionally turning a page and ruffling the sheets to straighten it back out.

"Hello! Sir?" Gabriel yelled as he knocked on the glass again. "May I please come in? I want to buy some comic books. I have money." Gabriel pressed the few crumpled dollars up against the glass.

The man behind the counter lowered his paper and for the first time Gabriel realized this was not Mr. Patrick. This man possessed a head of jet-black hair and a pair of icy silvery-blue eyes that glared at Gabriel from over the top of the page. "Read the sign," the man bellowed out before raising his paper back up.

"The sign?" Gabriel asked himself glancing up at the OPEN sign resting in the window. "The sign says open!" Gabriel hollered back.

"Try the other sign," the man replied from somewhere behind his newspaper.

Gabriel took a step back from the door and looked at the other sign that he somehow seemed to overlook in his excitement. This one was a long white sheet of paper with crimson print running down its face. It simply read,

NO LOITERING
NO BROWSING
NO WINDOW-SHOPPING
NO CHILDREN (without parent or guardian)
APPOINTMENTS PREFERRED

-the management. Wicked Books, Inc.

"Wicked Books?" Gabriel read the last line over again. What did that mean? Where was Mr. Patrick? Gabriel rapped on the glass again, but this time the man with the newspaper paid him no mind. Gabriel waited another minute or so, then ever so slowly he turned and walked back over to his bike.

Mounting his bike, Gabriel looked back at the storefront and that was when he first saw it. On the front of the building where the words, WONDER BOOKS had once stood, now had a new sign built over the old. The original "W" was still there but now the word WONDER had been replaced with the word, WICKED, creating a new sign which read, WICKED BOOKS.

"Wicked Books?" Gabriel said to himself, finally understanding a little more. His eyes darted over to the red sign that hung in the window. "No children?" he muttered to himself. "What kind of comic book store is this?"

Chapter Twelve:
FROM HERE TO THERE

"What do you mean you can't take me?" Gabriel yelled from across the kitchen table.

"Sorry, kiddo. But I need to work a double shift tomorrow." Gabriel's mother reached across the table and fumbled with the large salad bowl over-flowing with macaroni and cheese. "Maybe on Friday..."

"Friday?" A crazed gleam flashed across Gabriel's eyes. "That may as well be like, next year!" he fumed as he crashed back down in his chair.

"Acting like that isn't going to get you into that store any sooner, buster," Mrs. Woods added as she poured some Italian dressing over her salad. "Besides, I don't know if I even want you going into that store at all." She shook her head. "Wicked books? What kind of name is that for a comic book store? How do you know they even sell comic books in there with a name like that?"

"I know because I saw them," Gabriel replied in a huff. "I saw them through the window. Besides wicked might be a good thing. You know, like wicked cool, or wicked awesome." Gabriel tried his best to look cool as he spoke, but he came off a little goofy and awkward. Mrs. Woods simply stared at him blankly with a mouth full of salad.

"Yeah, well, like I said. Maybe on Friday," Mrs. Woods finally replied while chewing some cherry tomatoes.

Gabriel tried to figure out a way to make this work for him. For a mo-ment, he thought about telling his mother about the dirt and the message on his desk, but in the end he figured that would just be a little too weird on top of everything else that had been happening over the past few days.

"Are you going to finish eating? Or are you just going to keep slipping your extra food into your lap in hopes I won't notice?" Mrs. Woods asked dryly.

"You know, I wouldn't have to hide food in my lap if we had a dog," Gabriel replied. "I could just slip him the scraps from under the table."

"Oh, yeah. Brilliant logic there, Mr. Spock."

"Who?"

"Never mind." Mrs. Woods sighed as she scooped a large gloppy spoonful of macaroni onto a fresh plate and handed it to Gabriel. "Just bring this out to Grandpa Jerry and you're done."

"Cool. Thanks." Gabriel took the plate of fresh food and dumped the napkin full of half chewed macaroni (that he had been hiding in his lap) onto the table. Mrs. Woods just shook her head as she watched Gabriel open the front door and head outside.

It was only six o'clock, but it was already dark out. Gabriel yanked on the metal beaded chain and switched on the porch light. In an instant, a flock of large grey moths converged on the exposed light bulb knocking themselves against the glass over and over again. Gabriel quickly hopped down the weathered porch steps and began his way around the side of the house to the garage door.

Gabriel turned the corner and saw something that startled him so badly that the plate slipped from his hand and cracked in two on the ground. Standing in front of him was a large man in a red checkered shirt and denim overalls. The man's body was as thick as a wooden barrel and he stood with a slight hunch as if it was difficult for him to stand up straight. On his feet he wore enormous black rubber work boots with thick orange soles. His face appeared grizzled and leathery and his right eye was white and milky as if all the color had been drained from it leaving only the faint hint of where his pupil might be. The man turned and stared at Gabriel. A long piece of braided wire hung from his belt in a loop and the hundreds of keys that dangled upon it rattled as the man moved.

"Who are you?" Gabriel asked in shock.

The grizzled man smiled slightly revealing his gnarled yellow teeth. He took a step toward Gabriel, and as he moved Gabriel spotted a large metal trap hanging in the man's right hand. The grizzled man glared at Gabriel with his milky white eye; then spoke in rhyme.

"A-Hab's the name.
Hunting's my vice.
I'll find ya me darling.
And trap ya up nice."

The man spoke with a deep voice, and his thick Cape Cod accent led Gabriel to believe he wasn't a resident of Foxfield.

"Mom!" Gabriel yelled at the top of his lungs. Mrs. Woods quickly burst through the front door and ran out onto the porch.

"Hey you! Who are you?" Mrs. Woods demanded in an angry fluster.

The man looked up at Mrs. Woods for a moment, examining her in the porch light. Blinking, he looked back at Gabriel then finally spoke. "Sorry to spook ya ma'am. The name's Ahab, and yes I've heard all the Moby Dick jokes before so you can save 'em. My father was a whaler you see. It was his idea to name me the like."

"Gabriel come here," Mrs. Woods said sternly. Gabriel quickly scrambled back up the stairs and stood on the porch next to his mother. "All right Ahab, what are you doing here?"

The grizzled man hoisted his overalls up a bit. "Official business ma'am. I've been sent here by the city. Seems your town is having a bit of trouble with some vermin. That's where me and my little friends here come in." Ahab lifted up the metal animal trap that he was holding. The light from the porch glinted off the trap's razor sharp teeth. "Looks like you have a real problem with foxes. Apparently, this town hasn't seen this many red coats since the Revolutionary War." He laughed to himself as he spoke. Mrs. Woods didn't smile. "So your mayor has hired me to help thin their numbers if you know what I mean?"

Mrs. Woods glared at Ahab. "So you're a trapper. What are you doing here sneaking around my house at night?" Gabriel had never seen his mother like this. She seemed so strong. So forceful. And for some strange reason, it made him miss his dad even more.

Ahab reached into the large pockets of his overalls and fished around until he finally pulled out a pink sheet of paper. "This here's from city hall. I've been given free reign to set traps where I please and how I please to catch these foxes. You're the last house on my list. It took me all day to do most of the tracking you see. And it looks like most of the foxes are coming from right here. Under your very noses." Ahab pointed to Mrs. Woods and Gabriel.

"They are?" Mrs. Woods' tone suddenly dropped.

"That they are. From the forest." Ahab smiled. "I'd keep the boy clear of the tree line. I've set enough traps around there to kill every fox twice." Ahab then made a slitting motion under his throat. "It's funny though. To tell the truth, I've never seen anything quite like this."

"Like what?" Gabriel asked.

Ahab rubbed the thick prickly stubble that clung to his jaw. "I spent all day tracking the little devils, and well... it's almost as if the foxes are only interested in two places in this town. This old house here..." Ahab gestured to the farmhouse, "and a little brick bookstore over in the center of town. It seems crazy, but all of the tracks, and I mean all of them, seem to lead from here to there."

Chapter Thirteen:
LUNCH ON THE LAWN

Gabriel didn't sleep very well that night. His dreams were filled with foxes and locked doors. He also dreamt of strange messages written in the dirt and dark figures with ghostly white eyes that seemed to chase him endlessly in his sleep. When he finally woke up, Gabriel found that he had accidentally cocooned himself in his top sheet and had a very tough time wriggling free.

"Rise and shine, sleepy head." Mrs. Woods popped into Gabriel's room right on cue and helped unwrap him.

"So, you're sure you can't meet me at the comic book store after school today? Just for five minutes?" Gabriel tried his best to sound pathetic.

"No can do," Mrs. Woods replied cheerfully as she draped the sheet back over Gabriel's bed. "Someone here has to pay the bills. But, like I said last night, maybe Friday after work. Now, hurry up and get going, or you're going to be late for school!" Gabriel finished his morning routine and headed off to school.

As always, the school day seemed to move intolerably slowly. All through class Gabriel continued to ponder some way to get himself into the comic book store, if only for a few minutes. That way he could ask the new owner what happened to Mr. Patrick and maybe pick up a new comic book. It was then that he realized this was the longest he had ever gone without getting a new comic book. Maybe that's what was getting to him. Maybe there was no message in the dirt yesterday. Maybe he imagined it all. This could be his mind trying to make up for the lack of comics. Trying to entertain him. Distract him. Any way possible.

"Okay captain A.D.D., maybe you can tell us the answer to number eleven?" Mr. Silverman stood before Gabriel, math book in hand. He seemed to be looking at the crudely drawn fox doodles Gabriel had subconsciously been drawing in the lower margin of his textbook.

"Number eleven?" Gabriel snapped out of his daze.

"Yes. Can you please tell us the answer, Gabriel?" Mr. Silverman glared at Gabriel with a cocked eyebrow waiting for the answer.

Gabriel looked down at his textbook and quickly realized he didn't have a clue as to what they were talking about. Scanning the page, he didn't see any sign of question numbers. Turning back to Mr. Silverman, Gabriel shrugged and sheepishly ventured, "Twenty... seven?" The class all laughed.

Mr. Silverman frowned and glared at Gabriel for a moment. "Lucky guess," he grumbled and turned his attention back to the chalkboard.

Gabriel felt a wave of relief wash over him as Mr. Silverman changed the topic from math to history. For the remainder of the day, Gabriel decided it would be best if he focused on the lessons and not on the comic book store.

The lunch bell soon rang, and Mr. Silverman dismissed the class for one hour. On his way out, Mr. Silverman stopped Gabriel. "Don't forget today starts your after-school detention, Gabriel," Mr. Silverman reminded him.

"Oh yeah, right." In all the weirdness Gabriel had actually forgotten about that. "How does that work?"

"You'll get ten minutes after class to yourself, then you'll need to meet me back here," Mr. Silverman replied.

"Right, got it." Gabriel smiled and headed to his locker to get his lunch.

Sitting on the lawn, Gabriel watched as a number of men in orange hard hats worked on removing the enormous oak tree that fell on the night of the big storm. Some of the men were talking about how they had to order a large crane all the way from Natick.

Gabriel took a bite out of his baloney sandwich as he watched the men run cables under the tree and hook them up to the crane's winch. The sun seemed especially bright today and he had to shade his eyes in order to watch the men work. Suddenly a tall thin man wearing a red sport coat and blue jeans stepped in front of Gabriel blocking out the sun for a moment.

"Excuse me young man, but do you have the time?" The tall thin man asked Gabriel.

Gabriel wiped the ketchup from his mouth. "Sorry. I don't have a watch," Gabriel replied.

"Oh." The thin man looked overly disappointed. Gabriel noticed that the man was wearing a wristwatch. He wondered why he didn't just check his. The thin man seemed to be scanning the front of the school as if he were looking for something and didn't really seem interested in the time at all.

"Hey, Sally!" Gabriel yelled out to a gaggle of girls all sitting in a circle. The girls were busy trading stories and desserts.

"Yeah, what?" Sally called back, obviously a little embarrassed and surprised that a boy was yelling at her from across the lawn. The thin man also seemed surprised at this outburst and nervously began to fidget a bit.

"Do you know what time it is?" Gabriel hollered.

Sally looked at her watch and shouted, "It's twelve thirty four!"

"Thanks!" Gabriel replied. Turning to the tall lanky man, Gabriel smiled and took a bite out of his sandwich. "It's twelve thirty four."

"Oh, well thank you, young man." The thin man in the red sport coat seemed a little put off and shaken by Gabriel's exchange and quickly turned and walked off.

"Hey, mister," Gabriel called after the man. The stranger turned and looked back at Gabriel.

"Yes?" he replied.

"Why don't you just use your wristwatch?" Gabriel gestured to his own bare wrist.

The man appeared surprised by Gabriel's question and looked down at his wristwatch. "Oh. Um. This old thing?" the man began. "It hasn't worked for years. I just keep it for sentimental reasons." The man awkwardly smiled and waved as he continued to walk. "But thank you again, Gabriel."

Gabriel dropped his sandwich. "Hey!" Gabriel yelled out so loudly that the construction workers all looked over. "Hey you! How do you know my name?" Gabriel yelled at the thin man, but he was too late. The man had quickly vanished around the corner and was gone from sight.

Chapter Fourteen:
THE DEAL

Who was that man? How did he know my name? Was he someone Mr. Higby had sent to try and get my copy of Riley: Ace of the Skies? Gabriel rolled the thoughts around in his head as he sat all alone after school in Mr. Silverman's classroom. Things were definitely getting weird.

"Gabriel." Mr. Silverman entered the classroom and sat down at his desk. "I want you to sit quietly and read for the hour. Then you may go."

"Is that it?" Gabriel blurted, surprised by Mr. Silverman's orders.

"Do you need more to do?" Mr. Silverman asked sarcastically. Gabriel shook his head, no. Mr. Silverman rolled his eyes. "Listen, I want to get out of here as badly as you do, so just sit quiet and watch the clock. Got it?" Gabriel shook his head yes. "Good. This will prepare you for what it's like to work in the real world." Mr. Silverman reached into his satchel and pulled out a dog-eared copy of a sports magazine that featured an enormous image of the New England Patriots' Quarterback on the cover.

Well this was a good sign, Gabriel thought. It looked like Mr. Silverman wasn't really interested in punishing him. He didn't have to write lines, or study, or anything. All he had to do was sit quietly and read. Fortunately, Gabriel knew exactly what it was that he wanted to read. Opening his backpack, Gabriel plunged his arm deep inside the bag and resurfaced with a rolled up comic book clutched tightly in his fist. It was the recent issue of the armor-covered superhero, Ironclad.

As Gabriel opened the comic his olfactory senses were reminded what fresh printer's ink and comic paper smelled like. To him, it was Christmas, his birthday, and winning the World Series all wrapped up in one.

Gabriel began reading, and he was quickly reminded of all the action he was missing. This was a particularly good issue because it was the first time Ironclad (the man with the high tech bio-mechanical suit) and

Liberty Belle (America's female super soldier) were teaming up against the Doomsday Legion.

"What is that?" Mr. Silverman got up from his chair and walked over to Gabriel's desk.

"You told me to be quiet and read," Gabriel replied.

"I meant read a textbook. Or get a jump on your homework. That sort of thing. What is this anyway?" Mr. Silverman snatched the comic off Gabriel's desk. "Ironcloud?" Mr. Silverman grimaced.

"Ironclad," Gabriel corrected.

Mr. Silverman shot Gabriel a piercing glare. "Humph. I just don't get all this fantasy stuff. What do you see in this junk, Gabriel?"

Gabriel didn't really have an answer. "I don't know. I just like it."

Mr. Silverman quickly flipped through the pages. "You can have it back after detention. Now get out your English textbook and get a jump on tonight's reading assignment. You need to finish reading Johnny Tremain." Mr. Silverman returned to his desk and sat back down in his creaky chair. Gabriel reopened his backpack and removed his textbook. He looked crestfallen. "Cheer up Gabe," Mr. Silverman added seeing Gabriel's expression. "Tell you what; I'll let you in on a secret. There's going to be a pop quiz tomorrow on tonight's reading homework." Mr. Silverman smiled as he opened up his sports magazine. "So read up, and I'm sure you'll ace it."

Gabriel opened up his musty smelling textbook and scanned the pages until he spied his homework. However, he just couldn't bring himself to read it. Not while his comic book was sitting up there on Mr. Silverman's desk. Maybe there was some way to get it back.

"Knock. Knock." Both Gabriel and Mr. Silverman looked up at the same time. Standing at the open door was Miss Burke, the prettiest teacher in the school. She was tall and thin with thick blonde hair. Even Gabriel became a little nervous when she was around.

Mr. Silverman dropped his magazine and sat up straight in his chair. "Hello, Samantha," he stammered.

"Hello, David. I'm all out of staples." Miss Burke held up a large red stapler. "Can I borrow some from you?" she asked as she walked over to Mr. Silverman and looked down at him with her big blue eyes.

"Uh, sure." Mr. Silverman replied as he opened his desk drawer and fumbled around with its contents. "I know I have some more in here somewhere," he grumbled as he burrowed deeper into his desk.

"What's this?" Miss Burke reached down and picked up Gabriel's comic book.

Mr. Silverman glanced up from digging in his drawer. His face turned red. "Oh that."

"I didn't know you liked comic books, David." Miss Burke smiled.

"Well I..." Mr. Silverman began to answer but was cut off in mid sentence.

"I love comic books. Especially anything with Liberty Belle. I just adore her. I have ever since I was a little girl." Miss Burke opened up the comic book to a page where Liberty Belle was holding an armored car over her head. "I always wanted to grow up and be just like her, you know? Strong, beautiful and always ready to kick butt!"

Gabriel couldn't believe his ears, a teacher who liked comic books as much as he did! Could it even be possible? Why wasn't he in her class?

Mr. Silverman's eyes darted to the cover, and he took a moment before answering. "Yeah, well. I mean, she's great and everything, but she's no Ironclad," he coolly replied.

Gabriel's jaw dropped. He began to fume inside. Mr. Silverman was pretending to like comics just to impress Miss Burke. He thought about saying something to embarrass Mr. Silverman, but in the end figured that would be the worst thing he could possibly do.

"Wow, I never thought I would meet anyone who likes comics as much as I do." Miss Burke was smiling from ear to ear.

"Oh. Uh, yeah. Me, too." Mr. Silverman was now playing the moment for all it was worth. "Hey, would you like to have dinner with me tonight? We could talk about comics if you like." Miss Burke looked surprised at Mr. Silverman's question but continued to smile while she nodded, yes. "Great. I'll call you later this evening say about five o'clock?"

"Five sounds perfect," Miss Burke cooed, walking on air as she exited the classroom. As soon as she was gone, Mr. Silverman got up and quietly closed the door. He then picked up the copy of Ironclad and walked back across the room to Gabriel.

"Gabriel," Mr. Silverman began. "I'm going to make a deal with you, understand me?" Gabriel quietly nodded. "Good. Now listen very carefully. I need to know everything about these Ironclad and Liberty Belle characters by five o'clock tonight. I need you to make me an expert. Got it?" Again Gabriel nodded, yes. "Good. And in exchange for that, I'll let you blow off the rest of your detentions with me, but you can't breathe a word of this to anyone, especially the principal. Agreed?" Mr. Silverman held out his hand. Gabriel was dumbfounded. He had never heard a teacher talk to him like this before, and he wasn't certain how to reply. So he simply reached out and shook Mr. Silverman's hand.

"It's a deal, Mr. Silverman," Gabriel replied with a cagey smile. "And I happen know the perfect place for us to go do your homework."

Chapter Fifteen:
MR. WICKED

It was three thirty when Mr. Silverman pulled up to the front of Wicked Books in his beat up old car. Gabriel stood by his bicycle, waiting. With a slam of the car door, Mr. Silverman walked up to the storefront and looked over the façade. "This is the place you were telling me about?" he asked Gabriel as he removed his sunglasses and tucked them neatly into the pocket of his sports coat.

"Yup," Gabriel replied. "You should knock on the door. The guy inside just ignores me."

"Why is that?" Mr. Silverman asked. Gabriel pointed to the sign on the front door. Mr. Silverman read it over carefully. "It says you need an appointment? Who does this guy think he is? It's just a comic book shop!"

For once, Gabriel agreed with his teacher. "That's what I thought." Gabriel replied with a smile. Mr. Silverman tried the door, but it was locked. "Knock," Gabriel suggested. Mr. Silverman rapped on the glass with his knuckles. He then shaded his eyes and peered inside. Gabriel looked too. As far as they could see, no one was there but all the lights were on.

"Maybe he went out for a bite to eat?" Mr. Silverman shrugged.

"No. Look there." Gabriel pointed to the backroom where a slender man with raven black hair appeared and slowly strolled up to the front door with a skeptical look in his eye. The man turned the deadbolt and cracked open the door to examine them.

"What do you want?" the man asked in a questioning voice.

"I want to buy some comic books," Mr. Silverman replied.

"I see," the man murmured. "And do you have an appointment?" The words rolled snidely off his tongue as if he had rehearsed this meeting.

"No." Mr. Silverman seemed annoyed by the shop owner's line of questions.

"I see." The man flashed a devious smile at Mr. Silverman. "Well, I'm sorry, but I can't help you today. Maybe tomorrow if you schedule an appointment." The man began to close the door.

"Wait. I'll pay you double for the comics." Mr. Silverman wedged his shoe in the door jamb blocking it from closing.

"I'm sorry, but that's not how I do business," the man with the black hair hissed as he continued to try and close the door on Mr. Silverman's foot.

"Fine! Gabe, let's get out of here. I'll drive you to Mansfield to get those comics." Mr. Silverman turned and started marching back to his car. Gabriel felt his stomach lurch.

Suddenly the man stopped closing the door and turned to Gabriel like a serpent coiling to strike. "Gabe? Certainly, you're not Gabriel Woods?"

Mr. Silverman stopped walking. "How do you know his name?" he demanded.

The store owner ignored Mr. Silverman and continued to stare at Gabriel. "So you are Gabriel Woods! Very interesting indeed. Mr. Patrick told me everything about you." The man glared down at Gabriel with his piercing blue eyes and uneasy smile that made Gabriel's skin crawl.

"Oh, really? Did he?" Gabriel stammered. "Well... Um... that's cool. I guess."

"Why don't the two of you come in." The man with the raven hair opened the door wide and gestured for them to enter. "Let me introduce myself. I am Cornelius Wicked, the owner of this shop. I've been waiting to meet you Gabriel. I might have just the thing you're looking for."

Chapter Sixteen:
INSIDE THE STORE

"Well, that's more like it," Mr. Silverman grumbled as he stormed past Mr. Wicked and entered the store. Gabriel followed in Mr. Silverman's shadow as Mr. Wicked closed and locked the door behind them.

Looking around the store, Gabriel couldn't believe his eyes. Everything was different. The large wooden shelves were gone. In their place now were row after row of neatly aligned silver racks. Each rack seemed to hold an orderly line of individual comic books; each one wrapped in a sterile plastic baggy and spread out equal distance across the rows. There were no display racks, no baseball cards, and no toys. The only other items in the room were the front counter where the cash register rested and a rusty old wire rack where a few of the baby comics lay tattered and torn.

"What happened to the store?" Gabriel was white as a sheet.

"What do you mean, what happened?" Mr. Wicked snapped, mocking Gabriel's tone. "This is infinitely better than the way this dump used to be." Mr. Wicked walked out among the wire racks. "You see each of these comics is an extremely rare first edition. No two are alike." He ran his long fingers lovingly across the face of one of the comic books. "These are the best of the best and the rarest of the rare. A true comic book collector's store." Mr. Wicked strode up to Gabriel and looked him in the eye. "I'm surprised an expert of your caliber isn't more impressed."

"But where are all the boxes of comics that used to be up on the shelves?" Gabriel gestured to where the large wooden shelves used to be.

"They're all gone. I don't keep riff raff. I don't have time or room in my store for trash. So I tossed them with the rest of the garbage I found when I took over this shop," Mr. Wicked proudly remarked.

"So you don't have any Ironclad comics?" Mr. Silverman asked, beginning to look a little ticked off. Mr. Wicked paused for a moment and looked over at Gabriel.

"I might have what you need," he replied, all the while keeping his eyes on Gabriel. "I have Ironclad number one right here." Mr. Wicked broke his gaze and slid over to one of the far racks where he lovingly picked up a comic book trapped in a plastic bag. "But I may have something even better for you." Mr. Wicked spoke slowly, carefully enunciating each word. "Something that you could really use."

"And what would that be?" Mr. Silverman crossed his arms.

Mr. Wicked raised an eyebrow. "Why, Liberty Belle number one of course." Gabriel looked up at Mr. Silverman whose eyes were glazing over. "It would make a wonderful gift for that special someone, wouldn't it?"

"Yes. It would." Mr. Silverman replied softly. Gabriel couldn't believe what he had just heard. How did Mr. Wicked know about Liberty Belle when they came in looking for Ironclad?

"Would the gentleman care to see it?" Mr. Wicked asked Mr. Silverman in a coy voice.

"Yes. I would," again Mr. Silverman replied.

"I'm afraid that particular comic book is in a special room I keep in the back." Mr. Wicked smiled and gestured to the door leading to the back room. "It's far too important an item to keep out here on the shelves. But, if you wouldn't mind joining me in the back room for a moment I can show it to you there, Mr..."

"Silverman." Mr. Silverman replied as he walked towards the backdoor. "Wait here for me, Gabe. Okay? And for Pete's sake don't touch anything."

Mr. Wicked raised his palm and held it out in front of Mr. Silverman's face. "Wait. I'm afraid the boy can not stay in here unsupervised. He'll have to wait for you outside."

"What? I'll be fine waiting here. I used to practically work here you know," Gabriel protested.

"This is a store for serious collectors. Not a day care center," Mr. Wicked growled.

"It's his store, Gabriel. Wait out front, this won't take long." Mr. Silverman spoke in his teacher's voice at Gabriel.

"But..." Gabriel stomped his foot out of frustration.

"Rules are rules, lad." Mr. Wicked placed his hand on Gabriel's shoulder and escorted him to the front door. The man's hand was icy to the touch, and it sent a chill down Gabriel's spine.

"I'll be right out, Gabriel." Mr. Silverman waved as Mr. Wicked swept Gabriel out the front door and locked the deadbolt.

Gabriel peered through the glass and watched helplessly as Mr. Wicked led Mr. Silverman into the backroom and shut the door tightly behind them.

Chapter Seventeen:
NIGHTFALL

Gabriel sat on the stoop and waited. Looking through the glass window, he saw no sign of life within the store. How long had he been waiting? It felt like a long time. He wished he had a watch so he could check the time. That's when he remembered the strange man he had met at lunch. The thin man in the red sport coat. He knew Gabriel's name, and so did Mr. Wicked. For that matter, how did Mr. Wicked know about Liberty Belle? Maybe the man in the red coat was a spy for Mr. Wicked and not working for Mr. Higby after all. Maybe the stranger from lunch was listening in on Gabriel and Mr. Silverman's deal. Gabriel propped his head up on his hand and sighed. He had finally gotten into the comic book store, and he didn't get to buy a single issue. What a rotten day.

The shadows grew longer as the sun began to set. The glare on the window was gone now, and Gabriel could easily see inside the store. The lights were still on, but as far as Gabriel could tell, no one had come out of the back room yet.

What could be taking so long? Was Mr. Silverman reading the comics before he bought them? Or were Mr. Wicked and Mr. Silverman just talking shop?

The sun was definitely setting. The orange glare was in Gabriel's eyes, and he was beginning to get a headache. Maybe Mr. Silverman went out the back door. Was there a back door? Gabriel got up and strolled around the brick building. There was no back door, just a large green dumpster filled with black garbage bags and folded cardboard boxes.

"Okay," Gabriel mumbled to himself as he walked back around to the front of the store. Mr. Silverman's car was still there, the lights were on in the shop, but no one was visible inside. Gabriel knocked loudly on the glass door. "Hello!" he yelled. "Mr. Silverman? Are you still in there?" No answer. Gabriel stared at the flickering fluorescent bulbs in the ceiling. He pounded on the door, louder this time. "Mr. Silverman!" he shouted again at the top of his lungs.

Gabriel sat down and waited a little longer.

The streetlights were beginning to buzz on. Gabriel felt a cold wind blow as the sun slowly sank below the horizon. It was dark now. Gabriel didn't know what to do. Glancing around for any witnesses, he gave the glass door a good hard kick. "Mr. Silverman! Mr. Wicked! Are you still in there?" Gabriel cupped his mouth to the glass as he yelled.

No answer. Suddenly the lights within the store blinked off plunging the entire shop into total darkness. It was definitely night time now, and with the lights off within the store, Gabriel couldn't see anything at all. The only illumination came from the sickly green glow of the nearby street light.

Gabriel didn't know what to do. The store seemed more ominous now. Not the kind of place you wanted to be hanging around after dark. Then he thought back to Ahab's words.

"All the tracks lead from here to there," he said aloud to himself. The foxes. They could be there in the dark, just waiting for this opportunity to strike. Gabriel felt his throat go dry and his palms grow moist. He had to go home. Right now. Jumping onto his bike; he turned and looked back at the dark store. Mr. Silverman's car was still there, but there was no sign of Mr. Silverman himself.

Suddenly, a pair of hot white headlights filled Gabriel's eyes, blinding him for a moment. A car stopped fast in front of him kicking up a large cloud of dirt that swirled around in the light of the high beams. The car door opened, and Mrs. Woods stood up leaving the engine running. "Gabriel Winston Woods! You get in this car this instant! You are in big trouble young man!"

Even though his mother looked furious, and her eyes were practically glowing red, Gabriel was happy to see her.

Chapter Eighteen:
HURRICANE GLORIA

"I don't want to hear it!"

"But Mom!" Gabriel pleaded as Mrs. Woods drove her clunky little Japanese car home in the dark. "You have to listen to me. This is important."

"I don't want to hear it, Gabriel. You should have been home hours ago. I was worried sick. Do you have any idea what time it is?" Mrs. Woods growled.

"No, could you buy me a watch?" Gabriel suggested.

Mrs. Woods floored the gas. "Are you being smart with me, young man?" she snapped.

Gabriel shifted in his seat. His mother had jammed his bike into the car's tiny back seat, so the handle bars were poking him uncomfortably in the neck. "No. Please, I'm serious."

Mrs. Woods huffed loudly. "I don't think so, Gabe. You're not going to be needing a watch because you're going to come straight home after school from now on. No more comic book nonsense."

Gabriel knew he needed to straighten everything out. Tell his mother the truth about all of it. "But that's what I've been trying to tell you. It's Mr. Silverman. He took me to the comic book store today and..."

"Oh... oh! So I see how it is! You got your teacher to take you to the store because you couldn't wait until Friday for me to take you? Is that it?" Mrs. Woods blasted the car horn at nothing. "You are so grounded, mister."

Mrs. Woods swerved the car through the dark wooded street. "But Mom!" Gabriel moaned. "Please listen to me..."

"Not another word, young man." Mrs. Woods pointed at Gabriel with her free hand. "Not another word. You will come straight home from school tomorrow and that's final!" Mrs. Woods bellowed the words as the car pulled up in front of the farmhouse. Gabriel knew there was no arguing with his mother at this point. He would just have to wait out the storm until his mother came to her senses. Mrs. Woods wrenched the key killing the engine. "Now march upstairs, and go to bed this instant! And I don't want you reading a single comic book! Got it? Not one!"

Gabriel didn't answer her. He didn't want to provoke his mother any more. He simply wrestled his bike free from the back seat and lumbered up the stairs to his room.

Chapter Nineteen:
THE SAND FOX

Gabriel stood barefoot on the hot desert sand. The heat from the ground rose in waves distorting the horizon and making it difficult to breathe. Gabriel knew exactly where he was. He was looking out over the desert in his pajamas. He wasn't certain exactly which desert this was but he knew he was somewhere in the Middle East. It was all familiar to him because he had experienced this dream many times before. This was the dream where he watched his father die.

Looking out across the empty wasteland of scrub and dust, Gabriel could see a series of tents and trucks. Alongside those were five silver jet fighters glistening in the midday sun. The American flag flew on a pole nearby. Although he was far away, he could see the Air Force technicians in their orange jumpsuits working on the jets. Some of them were loading fuel. Others were towing out long green plastic cases that they parked alongside the planes. Then he saw him, his father. Gabriel watched as his father strolled around the plane a few times, occasionally brushing his palm against the exterior as he walked. He was performing his preflight check.

Gabriel was never certain why he always had this vivid dream. He wasn't there. He had never been to the Middle East. He was back in Foxfield with his mother and grandfather when his father was shot down. But there he was nonetheless, standing in the desert, having the same dream he'd been having for years.

Next came the film. Gabriel knew it all by heart. A technician came out of a nearby tent and loaded a large canister of film into his father's plane. You see, although Gabriel's father was a fighter pilot, his main job was to fly low over the enemy and photograph their base. These photos would later be developed and used by the army to help them pinpoint an attack from the ground.

Gabriel watched silently as his father donned his helmet and climbed into the cockpit of his plane. As the canopy closed, Gabriel could read his father's nickname painted on the side of the plane in bright red lettering. The Sand Fox. Then the plane slowly taxied into position, and once the ground crew gave him the thumbs up, he would ignite his engines and blast off into the clear blue sky.

The plane flew high into the sky so far and so fast that, in a matter of seconds, it was gone from sight completely. That would be the last time anyone would ever see Gabriel's father alive.

Gabriel sat down on the hot sand. He knew he would wake up from this dream soon, and then he would have to go to school. But for now, he was content to sit and stare at the clear blue sky in hopes that his father would return this time. Anything could happen. It was only a dream after all.

Chapter Twenty:
THE SUBSTITUTE

The next morning, Gabriel woke late; and after a few minutes, he had forgotten all about his dream. Stumbling down the stairs, he found no sign of his mother and no sign of breakfast. There was, however, a note.

Gabriel,

I already took care of Grandpa Jerry and went to work. Take an apple for breakfast, and come right home after school.

-Mom

Short and to the point, Gabriel thought. She must not be over last night yet. Popping the apple into his backpack, Gabriel mounted his bike and took off down the road to school.

Arriving at school, Gabriel was greeted with yet another surprise. Mr. Silverman was absent. In his place, sat a silver-haired old woman. The name, Mrs. Roland, was written on the chalkboard in long, loopy, cursive lettering.

"Excuse me, Mrs. Roland." Gabriel raised his hand.

"Yes... um..." Mrs. Roland glanced down at the seating chart in front of her before finishing her sentence. "Gabriel."

"Do you know what happened to Mr. Silverman?"

Murmurs rose up from the class. Someone threw a wadded up ball of paper at Gabriel's head. "Quiet, you jerk. We'll have it easy while he's gone," someone behind Gabriel whispered in his ear.

"Simmer down now, children." Mrs. Roland called out while banging her hand on the desk. "I don't know where your teacher has gone. But I'll be filling in for him until he returns." Gabriel sat up in his chair and looked out the window towards Wicked Books. He wondered if Mr. Silverman's car was still there. Maybe he should say something? "Now class," Mrs. Roland continued, "can someone please tell me where you left off in your English readers? I'm afraid your teacher left so suddenly that he didn't have time to prepare a syllabus."

The remainder of the day actually moved pretty quickly. Mrs. Roland wasn't a bad substitute, and Gabriel actually liked the way she would get distracted during the lessons and begin telling the students about growing up in Brooklyn and how today's children didn't appreciate how good they had things. Eventually, the bell rang and class was dismissed.

On his way to the bike rack, Gabriel was stopped by a familiar voice. "Excuse me, but aren't you the student who was in Mr. Silverman's classroom yesterday afternoon?" Gabriel turned around to see the beautiful Miss Burke standing behind him.

"Yes, I guess I was," Gabriel sheepishly replied.

"This may seem like an awkward question but, you don't know what happened to him do you?" Miss. Burke smiled politely and fidgeted a bit as she spoke.

Gabriel didn't know what to say. He couldn't tell her that Mr. Silverman vanished last night in the comic book store. That would just sound crazy. Looking up into Miss. Burke's big blue eyes, he had to tell her something. "I don't know. I left his class after detention." Gabriel figured that he wasn't lying. Both of those statements were true.

Miss Burke wasn't very good at hiding her feelings, and Gabriel saw her expression drop along with her hopes. "Well... If you see him, will you let him know I was looking for him?"

"Sure thing." Gabriel smiled

"Thank you," Miss Burke replied as she headed off down to the hall toward her classroom.

Climbing onto his bike, Gabriel sat for a moment and thought about what he should do.

On one hand, he had a lot of unanswered questions about the new comic book store and its owner. But on the other hand, he knew his mother would clobber him if he didn't go straight home. Reaching into his pocket, he pulled out a quarter.

"Heads, I go to the comic book store. Tails, I go right home," Gabriel said aloud as he tossed the coin high into the air. The quarter hung in the air for a moment then fell back to the dirt. Gabriel leaned over and found the coin. Tails. "Okay. I'll just ride past the store on my way home," Gabriel justified his actions to himself as he pocketed the coin and headed off towards the comic book store.

Chapter Twenty One:
THE SONG OF THE FOREST

It appeared to be business as usual at the comic book shop. The lights were all on, and the open sign was hanging in the window. Gabriel squeezed the brake on his handlebars and slowed down. Mr. Silverman's car was gone. So what happened to him? If he had left the store after Gabriel, then why didn't he go to work today? Gabriel tried to see if he could spot Mr. Wicked through the half drawn blinds, but it was no use. As far as he could tell, no one was in the store.

The rest of the ride home was uneventful. No storms. No foxes. No strange messages. No vanishing teachers. Just the quiet sounds of the forest and eventually his family's farmhouse. Gabriel got off his bike and walked up to the front door where he found another note waiting for him.

Gabriel,

I asked Grandpa to put this note here for you.
Take the paint bucket and brushes I left for you
in the shed and paint the fence. Also, try and
straighten out any of the crooked fence posts.

-Mom

Gabriel sighed to himself and headed out to the dilapidated wooden shed. There he found a bucket of white paint and an old paintbrush with a head full of ruffled and broken bristles.

He decided to fix the crooked fence posts first, then go back and paint it all at once. That way he wouldn't have to stop painting to fix the fence, and the whole job would go a lot faster. What Gabriel hadn't anticipated was the minefield of wild cucumbers that kept causing him to slip and lose his footing as he wrenched the posts out of the ground. Once he had aligned each post, he banged them back into their holes with a shovel.

It was already late afternoon by the time Gabriel had finished pounding the last fence post back into the hard soil. This job was going to take a lot more time than he had anticipated. Using a screwdriver, he popped the lid from the rusty old can and stirred the paint with a nearby stick. Dipping the paintbrush into the bucket, he began painting the fence and wondering if this was something that normal kids did. He began to feel a lot like Tom Sawyer, which he soon realized was one of the most dorky things he had ever thought and vowed never to think that way again.

Dusk soon fell, and Gabriel was pleased to find that he had just finished painting the final post. That was a good thing because he was rapidly running out of paint. Wiping the sweat from his brow, he snapped the lid back on the can and ran the paintbrush under the garden hose to clean it off.

Suddenly, Gabriel heard a strange sound coming from inside the shed. It was a sort of fierce rustling noise, like a trapped animal that was desperate to escape. Gabriel picked up the broken stick he had used to stir the paint and held it in front of himself like a samurai sword.

"Hey!" he shouted hoping to frighten whatever was in the shed into leaving. Gabriel picked up a large stone and hurled it against the side of the shed. Again, the violent clamor tore through the tiny wooden shed. Gabriel began to breathe faster. There was a loud creaking sound as the shed door slowly opened outwards on its rusty hinge. Peeking its nose out from the bottom of the shed door was another bright orange fox. However, this one was clutching the bloody remains of a white rabbit in its sharp needle like teeth.

The fox stared up at Gabriel. Gabriel's eyes became transfixed on the white rabbit's red, blood-soaked coat. Gabriel felt his heart race. Blood pounded through his ears as he tightened his grip on the stick. The fox simply looked at him for a moment, then, ever so cautiously, slipped past him carrying the remains of the rabbit off into the forest. Gabriel tried to follow it, but the fox quickly vanished into the autumn leaves that dotted the forest floor.

Gabriel dropped his stick to the ground. His palms were clammy and peppered with bark flakes. His heartbeat slowed down, and for the first time,

Gabriel thought he heard something, something very strange.

Venturing a step forward, Gabriel stood on the edge of the dark forest and listened intently. The sound was faint at first, then it slowly seemed to grow louder. It sounded like a woman singing? The voice echoed out from somewhere within the very heart of the forest. It was one of the most beautiful sounds Gabriel had ever heard, and for some reason he felt the sudden urge to follow the singing into the woods. The sun had almost set, and a thin veil of fog was beginning to cover the forest floor.

"Gabriel!" Gabriel was snapped out of his trance by his mother's voice. She placed her hand on his shoulder and knelt down next to him. "Gabriel sweetheart, what are you doing?"

"Huh? What?" Gabriel replied still feeling a little dazed and lightheaded. He looked around and was surprised to see that he was somewhere deep in the forest, somewhere he didn't recognize. It was completely dark now, like time had suddenly skipped forward half an hour and Gabriel hadn't noticed it. Mrs. Woods was looking wide eyed and worried. In her hand, she held a large plastic flashlight.

"You were walking off into the forest, Gabriel. Didn't you hear me calling you?" She asked while running her fingers through his hair. "Are you alright, honey?"

"Didn't you hear it, Mom?" Gabriel asked.

Mrs. Woods looked confused and concerned. "Hear what?"

Gabriel looked into his mother's nervous eyes and decided not to say anything that would worry her further. "Nothing, I guess."

Chapter Twenty Two:
FACE OFF

Friday was pretty dull. Mrs. Roland continued her lecture on the importance of hiding your money in your shoe while riding New York City's public transportation, and the clock seemed to move as slow as ever. There was still no sign of Mr. Silverman, and again, Gabriel had little news to tell Miss Burke when he met her in the hall after class. In fact, the only real surprise occurred when Gabriel found his mother waiting for him outside when the final bell rang.

"Mom? What are you doing here?" Gabriel asked as he walked his bike over to his mother's car.

Mrs. Woods was sitting on the hood of her car with her green coffee shop apron slung over her shoulder. "It's Friday, isn't it? Didn't I promise to take you to the comic book store today?" Mrs. Woods replied with a smile. "I'll have to make the time up tonight, but I figured you've been having a rough enough week and needed a little break."

Gabriel couldn't believe his ears. "Really? Wow, thanks!"

"Come on. Bike on ahead and I'll meet you over there." Mrs. Woods replied as she slid off the hood and climbed into the driver's seat. Gabriel hopped on his bike and took off like a shot. He couldn't believe his luck, and he couldn't help but think that things were really turning around for him.

Mrs. Woods arrived at Wicked Books minutes before Gabriel and was already reading the sign on the door. "Man, who does this guy think he is?" Mrs. Woods fumed. "No children. Appointments? No window shopping? You can't even see through the windows!" Mrs. Woods gestured to the dusty blinds that were halfway closed.

"Tell me about it," Gabriel replied as he dropped his kickstand.

"Maybe we should just go to Mansfield tomorrow. I think there's a baseball card shop there. Maybe they have comics, too?" Mrs. Woods began to reconsider.

"No." Gabriel snapped. "We've got to go in there. I need to know..." Mrs. Woods raised a curious eyebrow waiting to hear the end of Gabriel's sentence. "Um... something," he finally expelled.

"Something, eh?" Mrs. Woods replied with a cagey grin. "Alright kiddo, here we go." And with that, she rapped her knuckles on the door. There was a pause. Then Gabriel heard the sound of someone unlocking the deadbolt. The door opened just a crack, and the sleek form of Mr. Wicked peeked out from within the store.

"Yes. May I help you?" Mr. Wicked wrinkled his nose like he smelled something foul.

Mrs. Woods took one look at Mr. Wicked and rolled her eyes. "Yeah pal, you can," Mrs. Woods replied. "My son here would like to buy some comic books."

"Your son?" Mr. Wicked looked down and spied Gabriel. "Oh, Gabriel!" Mr. Wicked's eyes lit up with a cold fire. "It's good to see you again," he spoke through a creepy half smile.

"You two know each other?" Mrs. Woods appeared shocked.

"We were introduced the other day when he first visited my shop." Mr. Wicked replied.

"I see." Mrs. Woods glared at Gabriel. "So he's already bought some comics from you?"

Mr. Wicked pretended to pick at his fingernails while he spoke. "Oh no. I'm afraid the boy had to wait outside while his chaperone did some shopping."

"What happened to Mr. Silverman?" Gabriel asked.

"I haven't the foggiest." Mr. Wicked shook his head. "He left shortly after you. I assumed you left together."

"What?" Gabriel blurted. "He never left."

"What a strange thing to say!" Mr. Wicked sneered at Gabriel. "Of course he left. Shortly after you." Mr. Wicked spoke the last words slowly, emphasizing each syllable as he spoke.

"Well that was then, and this is now," Mrs. Woods interjected. "And we want to come in and buy some comic books." Mrs. Woods reached out and leaned against the door forcing it open. Mr. Wicked pressed his entire body weight against it forcing it back.

"I'm afraid that's quite impossible right now," Mr. Wicked grunted as he pushed back against Mrs. Woods. "I already have another appointment waiting. Maybe you could return next week?"

"But we're here now." Mrs. Woods also grunted as she pushed back against the door.

"There's nothing I would rather do than entertain you and your son; however, I already have a customer waiting." A vein began to pop out of Mr. Wicked's forehead as he strained against the door.

"Who? The invisible man?" Mrs. Woods growled not budging an inch.

Mr. Wicked's eyes flared at Mrs. Woods' comment, and in the blink of an eye, he simply backed up and stepped aside. Mrs. Woods didn't expect that move, and the force of her own weight caused her to crash face first through the doorway.

"No, not the invisible man." Mr. Wicked gloated over Mrs. Woods who was now sprawled out across the dirty tile floor. Gabriel walked into the store

after his mother and there, in the middle of the shop, was the oldest looking man Gabriel had ever seen. The old man was small and bent. His hair was
white and his skin was leathery. Brown spots covered his hands and a clear
plastic air tube ran from a clip on his nose down to a canister that attached at
his hip. "If you must know, his name is Mr. Sanders," Mr. Wicked triumphantly
hissed as he gestured to the old man. "And he has an appointment. Unlike
some people." Gabriel helped his mother to her feet. Mr. Wicked seized the
opportunity and grabbed them both by their arms and ushered them from
his store. "Now if you will excuse me." Mr. Wicked continued, "I need you to
leave my shop. Come back when you have an appointment! " A cruel smile
curled his lips as he spoke, "I'm a very busy man." And with that, the door
slammed shut and locked with a turn of the deadbolt.

Mrs. Woods dusted herself off. "Tomorrow, we go to Mansfield!" she
shouted at the top of her lungs. "I hear they have a better selection there anyway!"

"It's okay, Mom." Gabriel smiled. "It's cool."

Mrs. Woods bent down and hugged him. "I'm sorry, kiddo. I tried." She
shrugged.

"Thanks."

Mrs. Woods looked at her watch. "I need to get back to work. I'll meet
you at home tonight. Be home by sundown. Got it?"

"Got it," Gabriel replied. Mrs. Woods gave him a kiss on the cheek and
drove back off into town.

Gabriel stood and watched carefully until his mother drove completely
out of sight. He didn't want her to know what he was about to do. He had
decided that it was time to finally get some answers. He knew the only way to
find out what was really going on inside that comic book shop was to go in
alone, any way he could.

Chapter Twenty Three:
MR. SANDERS

A light drizzle was beginning to fall as Gabriel pushed up on his toes and balanced on the top of the rusty green dumpster behind Wicked Books. Lifting the heavy metal lid, he propped it up against the building's brick wall and climbed it like a ladder. Now the edge of the roof was almost within his grasp. Stretching his fingers, he tried desperately to grab it, but his fingertips only brushed the corner. It appeared that the roof was just out of reach.

Gabriel figured that the only way he was going to get some answers was if he found another way into the store, but as far as he could tell, the front door appeared to be the only way in or out. That's when he realized that the roof might have a hatch down into the shop, or at least an air vent that he could squeeze into. So now, Gabriel stood balancing precariously on the edge of the open dumpster lid, about twelve feet in the air with the roof just out of his reach.

Relaxing for a moment, he balanced himself by holding onto the brick wall the best he could. Then, with a look of fierce determination on his face, he crouched down and sprang into the air as high as his legs could launch him. Stretching his body as far as he could, his fingers found the edge of the roof and he dug in tight. His legs spun madly as he quickly scrambled up the side of the building while the lid to the dumpster crashed shut behind him.

Step one was complete. He had managed to get up onto the roof. Now for step two, getting into the store.

Gabriel scanned the rooftop, and at first glance, he thought he may have reached a dead end. As far as he could tell, there was nothing on the roof except for sun bleached gravel and tar paper. He didn't want to make too much noise (especially considering the big bang the dumpster had just made), so he carefully tiptoed across the roof in search of some type of air-conditioning vent. He didn't find a vent, instead his shoe brushed against a service hatch in the corner of the roof.

Tugging on the metal ring, Gabriel gently lifted the door and looked down into the shaft. All he could see below him was a small ladder made from welded pipes leading down into the darkness. The drizzle was definitely turning into rain, and Gabriel was happy to have found the entrance when he did. Climbing down the ladder, he silently closed the hatch behind him and descended into the store.

It took a few seconds for his eyes to adjust to the darkness. It looked like he was somewhere in the ceiling area of the comic book store. There were wooden planks everywhere that spread out over the ceiling tiles like small catwalks. Gabriel crawled along one of the planks on his hands and knees until he suddenly bumped into something.

Gabriel peered into the darkness. He was able to make out a row of what appeared to be cardboard boxes. It was still hard to see, and Gabriel rubbed his eyes in an attempt to make them adjust to the darkness faster. Ghostly outlines carved the edge of the boxes out of the darkness, illuminated by pockets of light from the room below. Gabriel squinted and attempted to read the scribbling on the side of the closest box. The writing on the box read, 1955: The Crimson League issues 1-50. Gabriel instantly recognized the handwriting on the box to be Mr. Patrick's. These were some of the original comic books from Wonder Books, but what were they doing hidden up behind the ceiling tiles? Did Mr. Patrick hide them there? Or was this something Mr. Wicked had done when he took over the shop?

Curiosity was definitely getting the better of him; and Gabriel decided that even though he was precariously balanced on one of the planks, he had to take a peek inside one of the boxes. Gabriel reached out and slowly lifted the lid of the nearest box. It was lined with hundreds of comic books. Gabriel squinted in the darkness and tried to figure out how many boxes there were. Fifteen? Twenty maybe? It was the mother lode! Apparently, Gabriel had inadvertently stumbled onto Mr. Patrick's secret stash.

"Excellent choice, Mr. Sanders, if I do say so myself." Gabriel heard Mr. Wicked's voice echo out through the ceiling, although he wasn't certain what part of the store the sound came from. "I think you will be quite pleased with that selection." The sound of Mr. Wicked's voice grew closer. As Mr. Wicked approached, Gabriel could also hear the muffled sounds of a man struggling to breathe and the noise of a respirator pumping.

"Yes." Gabriel heard a new voice, which he assumed belonged to Mr. Sanders. It was an ancient raspy sort of voice. "What do I do next?"

"Simply follow me into the next room, and all your questions will be answered my good man." Gabriel heard Mr. Wicked's voice again, but it was louder this time. They were definitely walking around somewhere just below him.

"What? In there?" Mr. Sanders coughed. The voices were moving away from him again, and Gabriel decided to crawl along one of the planks so he could hear better.

"Just have a seat, Mr. Sanders, and I will take care of the rest." Gabriel could hear Mr. Wicked's voice coo as he closed the door behind them. "Now then. Are you ready? You understand there's no going back now?"

"Yes," Mr. Sanders replied in a raspy cackle.

"Good. I'm looking forward to adding you to my collection." Mr. Wicked hissed the words so coldly that Gabriel felt his skin crawl. What did Mr. Wicked mean by his collection? Did he mean comics? Gabriel wished he could see what was going on.

"Will it hurt?" Mr. Sanders asked meekly.

"Not at all," Mr. Wicked continued. "In fact, I promise you, you will never feel more alive!"

Hurt? Collection? That was it. Gabriel had to know what was going on. He wedged his index finger under the corner of one of the ceiling tiles. Then lifted it ever so gently so as not to attract attention to himself. Peeking through the crack in the ceiling, Gabriel could only see the back of Mr. Sanders' head sitting in an old arm chair. From this angle he couldn't see much else, at least nothing interesting.

"Are you prepared, Mr. Sanders?" Gabriel could hear Mr. Wicked's voice from somewhere off to his right. He watched as Mr. Sanders nodded, yes. "Good," Mr. Wicked calmly replied.

"What do I do now?" Mr. Sanders asked in between breaths from his respirator.

"Simply open your comic book."

Gabriel wasn't too certain what happened next. It looked like Mr. Sanders reached down and picked up the comic book that was resting on his lap. Gabriel recognized the comic as a copy of The Pecos Kid, an old cowboy comic from the nineteen fifties. At first it looked like Mr. Sanders simply opened up the comic book. However, as the old man turned the first page, an enormous fireball exploded up from the pages of the book and filled the room with a blinding hot blaze. Sparks and thin spirals of flame spilled up through the cracks in the ceiling tiles.

Gabriel stumbled backwards, tripping over his own arms as he recoiled from the blast. The scorching power of the heat wave was too much, and Gabriel found himself tumbling backwards uncontrollably. His hand missed the plank and his body smashed through the flimsy ceiling tiles. He hit the ground hard, crashing to the store's floor, as the remains of the ceiling tiles crumbled down around him.

Chapter Twenty Four:
TRAPPED

Gabriel didn't know what to do. Did everyone just get burned alive? What happened? Suddenly the doorknob to the back room rattled and turned. Gabriel scampered across the floor and scrunched himself up into a tiny ball in the corner of the shop. He was scarcely hidden. The only thing blocking him from sight was one of the shiny aluminum comic racks and a few rows of books in plastic baggies.

The door to the back room opened. Gabriel watched as Mr. Wicked stepped out looking none the worse for wear. There was no smoke. No fire. No sign at all that just moments ago the entire back room had been engulfed in flames. In his hand, Mr. Wicked held Mr. Sanders' copy of The Pecos Kid. It, too, looked fine. There wasn't a scorch mark on it. As he exited the room, Mr. Wicked tucked the comic book neatly back into its plastic bag. Behind Mr. Wicked, Gabriel could see the empty armchair where Mr. Sanders had sat. There was no sign of Mr. Sanders anywhere.

Mr. Wicked's eyes darted around the store as he slowly closed the door to the backroom. "Oh dear," Mr. Wicked began speaking in an almost playful manner. "It appears that I have a rodent problem." He was looking up at the hole in the ceiling tiles. "A very large rodent problem by the look of things." He walked over to the nearest rack and gingerly placed the Pecos Kid comic back into the row. "Now how should I deal with vermin like you? First things first, I suppose. I wouldn't want you to escape, now would I?" Mr. Wicked flicked his wrist and the dusty old blinds hanging on the front windows snapped shut so tightly that it blocked out all the light from the sun. "But you are a slippery one, aren't you? And you've narrowly escaped me many times past." Mr. Wicked moved his hand through the air and the front counter was suddenly wrenched loose from the floor. It slid across the ground and slammed against the front wall blocking any way to escape. "Hum. It looks like you're not hiding behind the counter." Mr. Wicked tapped his lips with his finger as he spoke. "Now, now. I know you're here somewhere. Don't think because I'm in this sickening mortal form I can't tell you're here. I can smell your blood, you know."

Gabriel felt his heart racing. He tried as hard as he could not to move. Not to breathe. He thought he might throw up.

"Let's see, am I getting warmer?" Mr. Wicked took a step into the center of the room. He looked over all of the comic book racks and then back up to the ceiling? "No? Colder perhaps?" Gabriel covered his mouth to try and muffle his breathing. Mr. Wicked took another step closer to him. Gabriel could see Mr. Wicked's shoes from between the comic books. "It's only a matter of time until I find you," Mr. Wicked gloated as he began to walk down the aisle next to Gabriel. "How about now? Warmer? I certainly feel warmer." Mr. Wicked's velvet tones made Gabriel's skin crawl. "Am I... burning up?"

Again, Mr. Wicked flicked his wrist, and fiery orange bolts shot from his fingertips. They struck his cash register melting it into a glob. "Not there either? I despise playing these games," Mr. Wicked called out into the room. "They belittle us both you know."

Suddenly, the telephone rang. At first, Mr. Wicked twitched as if he might fire another shot but caught himself halfway through. Striding over to the phone, he snatched up the receiver. "Hello, Wicked Books," he hastily spoke into the phone, all the while scanning the room for any sign of motion.

Gabriel didn't move. His legs were beginning to cramp up and ache, but he didn't dare move a muscle.

Mr. Wicked's tone sounded surprised, and for an instant it appeared he was no longer concerned with Gabriel. "Oh, you're back already? That was fast. I'll be right over. Goodbye." Mr. Wicked hung up the receiver and slid the counter back to where it belonged. "You're in luck today, my furry little friend. My niece is in town, and I must go see her." With a wave of his fingers, the blinds flew wide and the deadbolt snapped open. Overcast sunlight filled the room. Gabriel closed his eyes. He was certain Mr. Wicked was going to spot him. However, Mr. Wicked didn't see Gabriel. In fact, he didn't even bother to look. He simply plucked his coat from the rack in the front of the store and unlocked the door. "Until next time, my little rodent," he spoke as he strode out the door. The deadbolt snapped tight behind him.

Gabriel continued to lay on the floor scrunched into a tiny ball. He didn't want to move. It may have been a trap to lure him out of hiding, and he didn't want to risk it.

Gabriel stared at the clock and waited. Twenty minutes passed before he finally summoned up enough courage to stand up. His legs were killing him. Pins and needles shot through his thighs. He decided not to waste any time, and he hobbled to the front door, but try as he might, he was unable to turn the deadbolt to unlock it. Gabriel carried himself on his sleepy legs to the door to the back room but that, too, was now locked tight. It looked like the only way out would be the way he came in.

Gabriel placed a foot on one of the metal comic book racks and carefully began climbing. It actually wasn't that bad. The racks were strong, and Gabriel was so light that he barely bent any of the metal shelves. Reaching the ceiling, Gabriel slid aside one of the tiles and found the wooden plank beyond. He hoisted himself back up onto the catwalk and pushed the tile back into place with the toe of his shoe. Within a matter of minutes, he was back up on the roof. The rain cloud must have passed over while Gabriel was in the shop because the roof was now covered in deep puddles of water.

Gabriel walked across the sun-bleached gravel to the roof's edge where the dumpster lay below. From this height, the big green dumpster didn't look so big, but Gabriel decided that if he could get himself up here, he could definitely get himself back down. He just had to jump. It was the only way. Taking a deep breath, he bent his legs and jumped nimbly from the rooftop to the top of the dumpster below. Gabriel's feet landed square; however, he hadn't anticipated just how slippery the grimy painted metal could be (especially after the rain) and his feet flew out from under him. With a loud bang, he struck his head hard on the side of the dumpster and tumbled sideways onto the bags of trash dotting the ground. He couldn't see straight. Everything was blurry, and after a moment it all began to fade to black. The last thing Gabriel remembered before passing out was the cool sensation of the October rain drops hitting his face. Then, all went dark.

Chapter Twenty Five:
VOLE

"Excuse me, but are you alright?" Gabriel could hear a man's voice speaking to him. He still couldn't see straight and there was a ringing sound in his ears. It felt like there was a freight train thundering through his skull. Gabriel slowly opened his eyes. Everything was still a little blurry, but he could make out the shape of someone standing over him. "There you go. It looks like you're going to be all right. You took a pretty nasty fall." He felt the man pick him up and lean him against the side of the dumpster. Gabriel rubbed his eyes and the blurriness soon cleared. Standing before him was the strange man he had talked to the other day at lunch, the man in the red sport coat and blue jeans, the man that had run away from him when he called after him. "Don't worry," the stranger spoke calmly. "I'm not going to harm you. Quite the opposite in fact." The man smiled.

"What do you mean by that?" Gabriel asked as he rubbed the lump forming on the back of his head.

"I'm here to help you, Gabriel. You see, you seem to have gotten yourself tangled up in something that is... well..." The man stopped and tried to compose his thoughts. "Shall we just say, a little out of your league."

"Out of my league?" The disorientation was beginning to wear off. Unfortunately, the headache was here to stay. "Who the heck are you?"

"You may call me, Vole." The man replied with a slight bow.

"Vole?"

"Yes. Vole." The man nodded.

Gabriel frowned. "That's a pretty weird name. And you want me to trust you?"

"Yes," Vole replied. Gabriel got to his feet. As he stood up, his head began to throb, and he had to hold onto the slimy dumpster to regain his balance. "Be careful. You hit your head pretty hard."

"Ya think?" Gabriel snapped. Vole didn't react to Gabriel's comment. "How do you know my name, anyway? Do you work for that Higby guy?"

"Higby guy?" Vole repeated questioningly.

"I guess not," Gabriel muttered. He needed to get home, take an aspirin and put an icepack on his head. "So how did you know my name?"

Vole smiled. "I know everything about you, Gabriel. You see, it is my task to watch over you and protect you."

"Oh yeah? You're doing a real good job." Gabriel pointed to the lump on the back of his head.

"Well, I can't protect you from yourself," Vole shrugged. "But I can protect you from other things."

"Protect me from what?" Gabriel asked.

Vole looked toward the comic book store. "From him."

"Mr. Wicked?" Gabriel asked. "Then how come you didn't bust in there a minute ago?"

"Actually, it was more like an hour ago. You've been knocked out for a while-"

"Whatever!" Gabriel huffed and shook his head. "How come you didn't save me then?"

"I was unable to. He had protections against entry to my kind."

"Your kind?" Gabriel was getting confused, and this conversation wasn't helping his headache. "Listen, Dole..."

"Vole."

"Vole. Whatever. I don't have time for this. I need to get home." Gabriel began walking around the building to the front of the store where his bike was waiting for him. The sun was beginning to set, and he didn't want to make his mother angry, especially after she was so nice to him this afternoon. Vole trailed after him.

"Gabriel, listen to me. It is vitally important that you never go back into that store again. Do you understand me?" Vole's voice was soft, yet serious.

"I'm way ahead of you pal. I'm never going anywhere near that store again, for the rest of my life," Gabriel replied as he mounted his bike.

"Good."

"Nice meeting you, Vole," Gabriel added, and he began to pedal away.

"Gabriel, wait!" Vole shouted after him.

Gabriel stopped. "What now?"

Vole ran up beside him. At first, Gabriel was surprised at how fast Vole seemed to move. Maybe his eyes were still playing tricks on him. Vole stopped in front of Gabriel and looked into his eyes.

"I want you to listen to me very carefully, Gabriel Woods, because I am here to help you. This may not be over yet. I'm not certain why, but there is something about you that has piqued his interest. I will continue to try and figure out what he is planning. However, in the mean time, if you ever need my help all you need to do is go to the old covered bridge in the middle of the woods and call my name. Do you understand?" When he was done speaking, Vole smiled and raised his eyebrows. Gabriel simply crossed his arms.

"Listen, Vole," Gabriel began. "I don't know anything about you. You are one strange guy, and there is no way I'm going to go into the middle of the woods and talk with you alone at the covered bridge. So whatever you're up to, forget about it." Gabriel began to ride away leaving Vole in the dust. "And if I ever see you again," Gabriel added, "I'm telling my mom and calling the cops!"

Chapter Twenty Six:
THE INVITATION

Gabriel's head hurt for the remainder of the day, and he had almost no appetite. As an excuse, he told his mother that he had wiped out on his bike while riding home and hit his head on the sidewalk. That night in bed, Gabriel made a very tough decision. He decided that he would never set foot in his favorite comic book store again. He would have to wait and go to Mansfield with his mother and only buy comic books once a month instead of every day. That thought didn't help him fall asleep any faster, and his throbbing head kept him awake for most of the night. When he did sleep, he had nightmares of fireballs and foxes. The next day was Saturday and since there was no school, Gabriel asked his mother if he could just take it easy and rest his head. By late afternoon, he was feeling better.

"How's the old noggin doing?" Mrs. Woods asked Gabriel over dinner.

"Better," Gabriel replied as he cut himself a thick slice of meatloaf. "It still hurts to touch."

"Maybe we should go see the doctor?" Mrs. Woods suggested as she buttered her bread.

"No. I think I'll be okay." Gabriel didn't like going to the doctor. They always seemed to just prod him and stick him with pointy objects, all the while saying lame things like, "Hum." and "Interesting."

"Any thoughts about what you want to be for Halloween?"

To be honest, in all the weirdness of the past few weeks, Gabriel had forgotten all about Halloween. "I don't know yet. But I'll think about it."

"Better think fast, buster. You remember what happened last year," Mrs. Woods replied while eating.

Last year, Gabriel couldn't decide between being an astronaut or a vampire. He had waited too long to pick out a costume, and in the end, they were sold out of both. So, his mother made him a robot costume from an old trash can they had laying in the yard. All night long, the other kids kept trying to stick their empty candy wrappers in his mouth.

"Yeah. I remember," Gabriel grumbled.

The rest of the weekend was also pretty uneventful. Once or twice, Gabriel thought about telling his mother what had happened after she left Wicked Books on Friday. In the end, he decided that she would just get upset and he would get into trouble for breaking into the store.

Soon enough, Monday came and Gabriel returned to school. This time, he went out of his way to avoid Wicked Books and biked the long way around the town square. Eventually, Gabriel made it to class and took his seat.

"Good morning, class. It's good to be back." Gabriel's eyes went wide as Mr. Silverman strode into the room. He looked different. The drab white shirt and black tie he usually wore were gone and he was dressed in a bright blue sweater with khaki pants. He actually looked kind of cool.

"Mr. Silverman! Where were you?" A girl named Jessica called out.

Mr. Silverman tossed his car keys onto his desk. "I got married, children," he said with a smile, and held up his left hand. A gold ring was wrapped around his finger.

"You got married?" Gabriel blurted out.

"What Gabriel? Didn't think I had it in me?" Mr. Silverman glared.

"No. It's not that–" Gabriel stammered.

"Quiet down. I'm sure we have a lot of catching up to do. Will you all please open your math books, and pass forward the homework assignments I left for you." Mr. Silverman sat down at his desk and opened the drawer to remove his teacher's math book. "Oh. Gabriel. I believe this is yours." Mr. Silverman pulled out Gabriel's Ironclad comic book and handed it back to him.

"Uh. Thanks," Gabriel replied as he took the comic. On the back of the book Gabriel found a yellow post-it note. There was a message from Mr. Silverman.

Gabriel,

Please stay after class. There's
something I need to ask you.

-Mr. Silverman

Mr. Silverman gave Gabriel a friendly wink to let him know that he wasn't in trouble. The remainder of the afternoon went well. Mr. Silverman's good mood seemed to last throughout the entire day. He even decided to cancel homework for the entire class in celebration of being a newlywed.

Eventually, the final bell rang and the students began shuffling out of the classroom. Gabriel pretended to take an extra long time packing his backpack and watched out of the corner of his eye for the last student to leave.

"What's up, Mr. Silverman?" Gabriel asked as he walked up to the front desk.

"Gabriel, I wanted to thank you for all your help last week. And to show my appreciation, my new wife Vanessa and I would like to invite you to a spaghetti dinner tonight at my house." Mr. Silverman smiled as he spoke and wrote out a note on his teacher's letterhead. "Here." He tore the top sheet off the pad and handed the note to Gabriel. "Take this to your mother so she knows that I've invited you."

Gabriel looked over the note. "Are you sure, Mr. Silverman? You don't need to thank me. To be honest, I don't even know what I did. What happened to you that night? You never came out of the store."

Mr. Silverman smiled and laughed to himself. "It's a great story. I promise I'll tell you all about it over dinner tonight. Will you join us?"

Gabriel fidgeted for a moment. He wasn't sure what to say, but he had to find out what happened the other night when Mr. Silverman vanished without a trace. "Okay. I'll be there. What time?"

"Seven o'clock. I can't wait to tell my wife. She's excited to meet you and thank you herself." Mr. Silverman sat back in his chair and spun his pencil between his fingers. "I promise you, Gabriel, it will be a night you won't soon forget."

Chapter Twenty Seven:
MRS. SILVERMAN

Unfortunately, Gabriel was unable to tell his mother about the invitation. She had to work late, so he left the note with Grandpa Jerry and asked him to give it to her when she got home from work. Around six thirty, Gabriel got on his bike and headed off to Mr. Silverman's house. It was completely dark out when he left, so he decided to duct-tape his mother's flashlight to the handlebars of his bike so he could see his way in the dark.

It was a little before seven when Gabriel pulled up to Mr. Silverman's door and parked his bike by the mailbox. Mr. Silverman lived in a small one story house out near the edge of town. It was a nice house, small, but nice. As Gabriel approached the front door, he noticed a strange looking jack-o-lantern flickering on the doorstep. At first glance, it looked just like any other jack-o-lantern, but upon closer inspection Gabriel noticed that instead of a scary face, there was a word carved into the front of the pumpkin. The word, VULPES, was carved in large jagged letters in the face of the pumpkin. A flickering candle cast the word across the threshold of the porch. Gabriel didn't know what the word meant, but he figured it was just some egghead thing that Mr. Silverman decided to do in place of carving a spooky face. He was a teacher after all.

Gabriel pressed the doorbell and waited. It took a moment, but eventually Mr. Silverman opened the door with a smile. "Gabe, good to see you. I'm glad you made it. Come on in, we've been waiting for you." Mr. Silverman took Gabriel's jacket and hung it up in the hall closet. "I'm so glad you decided to come, Gabriel. I've been telling my new wife all about you and how we would have never met without your help.

"Honey? Is that our guest?" Gabriel heard a lovely woman's voice echo out from the kitchen.

"Yes, it is love," Mr. Silverman called back. Gabriel took a deep breath, the aroma of delicious home cooked food wafted in from the kitchen and it made his mouth water. "Why don't you come say hello?"

"What a wonderful idea," the woman called back as she entered the hallway from the kitchen. The tall thin silhouette of a young woman filled the hall. "Hello there, dear. I'm Mrs. Silverman, but you can call me Vanessa." Suddenly, Mrs. Silverman came into the light of the hallway.

Gabriel gasped.

Mrs. Silverman was a tall woman with a sleek figure and long raven black hair that fell to her waist. She wore a brown dress and black high heeled boots on her feet. But what made Gabriel gasp wasn't her clothes or her shape. It was the fact that the woman was missing her face! She had absolutely no facial features. There wasn't a mouth, or a nose, or even eyes. All she had was smooth, pearl white skin from her chin to her forehead. In place of her eyes, she had two large black beetles that scampered around where her eyes should have been, giving her the creepy appearance that she was looking at you. She held out her hand for Gabriel to shake, "Well, aren't you going to say hello?" Since she didn't have a mouth, her chin just moved around as she spoke and her beetles seemed to give her the appearance of glaring at Gabriel. Gabriel wiped the sweat from his palm and shook her hand. Her hand was freezing cold to the touch, and Gabriel felt his skin crawl as he shook it.

"Pleased to meet you," Gabriel mustered.

"Same to you, young man," Vanessa replied. Her beetles scurried around until it appeared as though she was looking at Mr. Silverman. "You were right, dear," she continued. "He is a charming fellow. He's going to be a real heartbreaker. I can tell." She then leaned over and kissed (even though she lacked a mouth) Mr. Silverman on the cheek.

Mr. Silverman gave her a tight squeeze. "What do you think, Gabriel? Isn't she the most beautiful woman on the face of the planet?" And he returned her kiss.

"She's uh... really something," Gabriel stammered.

"Oh, aren't you sweet. I could just eat you alive!" Vanessa bent over and leaned into Gabriel's ear. She was so close that he felt one of the beetles flutter its wings against his cheek. "I'm going to make you something extra special for dinner tonight," she whispered. Gabriel shivered. "Well, back to the kitchen for me," Vanessa declared. "I could use a big strong hand getting everything on the table, dear." Vanessa grabbed Mr. Silverman by the arm and pretended to squeeze his non-existent muscles.

Gabriel wanted to leave. He tried to think of an excuse to go, but he couldn't stop looking at Vanessa's head. Her beetles seemed to be constantly looking at him, even when she turned around.

"I have an idea. Why don't we leave Gabriel with your uncle, dear?" Mr. Silverman suggested. "Then, I can help you with dinner. Besides, I think the two of them will have a lot to talk about."

"Your uncle?" Gabriel asked.

"What a smashing idea, love. He's right in the next room, and I'm sure he would love the company while we set the table." Vanessa grabbed Gabriel with her icy cold hand and led him into the living room.

A fire was crackling in the fireplace, and it filled the room with a warm cozy feeling. There were two large armchairs facing the fireplace, and a man sat snugly in one of them. His back was to Gabriel, but from the moment he saw him, Gabriel knew exactly who the mystery man was. "Uncle, dear. There's someone I would like you to meet," Vanessa spoke as she entered the room.

The man in the chair turned around and smiled a twisted smile. "Don't be silly, my dear. No introductions are needed. Gabriel and I are old friends by now. Aren't we, Gabriel?"

Chapter Twenty Eight:
THE RAREST COMIC IN THE WORLD

Mr. Wicked sat in the high backed chair closest to the fireplace. "I'm pleased to see you again so soon, Gabriel. There's so much I want to talk with you about. Please, have a seat." He gestured to the empty chair across from him.

"I knew you two would be fast friends!" Mrs. Silverman squealed with delight. "I'll have dinner on the table lickety split." Her black beetle eyelids fluttered as she tugged on Mr. Silverman's arm and led him away towards the kitchen.

Gabriel and Mr. Wicked were now all alone in the room. Again, Mr. Wicked gestured to the chair across from him. "You may as well take a seat, Gabriel. She'll be a while. She's a terrible cook, you know," he added in a whispered tone. Gabriel cautiously walked over to the chair and edged his way onto the seat cushion, all the while keeping his eyes locked on Mr. Wicked. "You don't have to worry about me, son. I'm harmless. I just want to make you an offer. The most fabulous offer you will ever receive in this lifetime."

Gabriel felt the hairs on the back of his neck rise one by one. Was Mr. Wicked playing a game with him? "What do you mean, an offer? What kind of an offer?"

A crooked smile curved around Mr. Wicked's lips. "Let's not play games here, Gabriel. You're the whole reason I came to this pathetic little town in the first place. And once I have what I want, I will leave this town."

Gabriel didn't have any idea what Mr. Wicked was talking about, but he decided he had better keep him talking. "So, what do you want?"

"Why, Riley: Ace of the Skies, of course." Mr. Wicked looked around as if he were making sure no one was listening in. "You see, Gabriel, I'm quite a connoisseur of comic books. I only collect the absolutely most unique comics that have ever been printed, and I'm afraid you own the absolute rarest comic in the world."

"I do?" Gabriel was surprised. He knew his copy of Riley: Ace of the Skies was rare and valuable, but he had never imagined that he owned the rarest comic book in the whole world.

"Yes. You see, you own the first printing of the first edition of that particular comic. A comic that only had one printing in England during the blitz bombings of World War Two, and the factory was burned down by Nazi bombs after the first shipments had been sent. So, no other copies were ever produced. On top of that, no other number one issues seemed to survive the war." A hungry glint filled Mr. Wicked's eyes. "You, my boy, have the only copy in existence, and it is the number one of number ones. The most precious comic in world."

"Wow." Gabriel's eyes were wide. For some reason, he believed Mr. Wicked's story.

"Wow, indeed." Mr. Wicked smiled and flashed his ivory teeth. "And I want to make you a very special offer for it. Now, I know many suitors have come to you over the years with offers of money or trades, but I'm going to offer you something that no one else can match." He pointed his long boney finger at Gabriel as he spoke.

"And what would that be?" Gabriel cautiously asked.

Mr. Wicked collected himself and took a sip of tea. "Look on the table next to you."

Gabriel looked over at the small hand carved end table. On the table top rested a comic book in a plastic baggy. Gabriel picked it up and looked at the cover. It was a copy of The Eternal Guardian: Earth's Greatest Hero. It was a very famous issue, the one where the Guardian faces off against Gladicus Rex, the most powerful villain in the universe. Gabriel owned a cheap reprinting of this issue that was made on the comic's twenty fifth anniversary. Original ones were hard to find because it was the issue where the Guardian finally beats Gladicus Rex once and for all but loses his secret identity in the process. "Is this a real copy?" Gabriel asked as he flipped it over. On the back was an old advertisement for Boy's Life.

"Oh, it's real alright." Mr. Wicked chuckled to himself.

"So you want to trade my copy of Riley for this?" Gabriel asked.

"Not exactly," Mr. Wicked replied.

"Then what?"

"Open up the comic book, my boy. Take a look inside," Mr. Wicked replied dryly. Gabriel's face went white as a sheet. He recognized that tone of voice. He had heard Mr. Wicked speak those very words to Mr. Sanders right before the comic shop filled with fire. "What's the matter? Don't you want to open it up and take a look at it?"

Gabriel felt his sweaty palms glide across the face of the plastic bag. "Uh. No, that's alright. I know the story. I have a reprint of it they made last year."

Mr. Wicked shook his head. "Open the comic book, Gabriel. I insist."

"That's alright."

"Open it. Now." Mr. Wicked growled the words and Gabriel felt a cold wave wash over him. He thought back to the supernatural acts he had witnessed Mr. Wicked perform back in the comic book shop and figured it wouldn't be good to make him angry. Looking down, he flipped the comic over and slid the book out of the bag. "Now, open it." Mr. Wicked raised an eyebrow. "I think you will be pleasantly surprised."

Gabriel held the comic book gently in his hands. A strong smell of mothballs wafted up from the cover and Gabriel could tell that it was very old. The paper was light and thin, as if many hands had held this particular issue and read over it time and time again. Gabriel's hands trembled slightly as he began to turn the page. He didn't want to open it, but Mr. Wicked stared at him with such a piercing gaze that he felt he had little choice. Thumbing the cover, Gabriel opened the comic book.

The room filled with a blazing fireball that exploded up from the pages of the book. Clutching the comic with all his might, Gabriel screamed as the fire roared up from the page and engulfed him. The entire room was set ablaze, but Mr. Wicked sat across from Gabriel looking as cool as could be, still sipping his tea as the chamber became flooded with a brilliant orange light. It was becoming harder and harder to see, and as the heat of the fire enveloped him, the last thought Gabriel could muster was, "Oh no... what did I just do?"

Chapter Twenty Nine:
THE GUARDIAN

Gabriel closed his eyes. The heat was incredible. Then as suddenly, as it had begun, it ended. The fire was gone and so was the living room.

Gabriel found himself standing on top of a tall building in some type of enormous city. It was no longer night time. A clear blue sky filled the horizon, and a cool breeze was blowing in from the ocean. Gabriel looked at the skyline and couldn't help but feel that he recognized the buildings. He was somewhere familiar, but he couldn't quite place it.

What had happened to Mr. Silverman's living room? Where was he? He felt like he had seen this skyline a million times before, but where? Then he spotted it. The tallest building in the city. It's spire like shape was unmistakable. It was the Liberty Tower. Then everything became clear. Gabriel was in The District of Columbus, the home town of The Eternal Guardian. He was actually there. Gabriel was now (somehow) in the comic book he was just holding. Looking at his clothes, Gabriel couldn't believe his eyes. He was wearing a black and gold uniform with a long flowing cape and goggles. Then it dawned on him, he wasn't just in the Eternal Guardian comic book, he was The Eternal Guardian.

"Whoa," Gabriel expelled as he checked himself out. He felt amazing. He had never felt so alive in his entire life. He felt like he could do anything. Maybe even fly.

"Pretty fantastic, wouldn't you say lad?" Gabriel heard a familiar voice echo up from behind him. Turning around he spotted Mr. Wicked perched on a nearby rooftop. He was still in the same clothes he was wearing in Mr. Silverman's living room.

"What is this place? Where am I?" Gabriel shouted out to Mr. Wicked.

"Why, I would assume you of all people would know where we are, Gabriel." Mr. Wicked grinned sheepishly. "Or, I should say, Guardian."

"So, I am the Eternal Guardian?"

"That you are, lad. You have all of his powers. This world is the world of The Eternal Guardian. I'm afraid this is all very real indeed."

Gabriel couldn't believe it. "How did you do this?"

Mr. Wicked shook his head. "I didn't do this. You did this. This is one of your dearest innermost desires." Mr. Wicked pointed to Gabriel. "You made this happen. I simply showed you the door. Here, in this place, almost all of your most precious wishes, your hopes and your dreams can come true. You, Gabriel Woods, are now The Eternal Guardian."

Suddenly, a loud blaring siren shook the streets. Gabriel recognized that noise. It was the Guardian's call, which meant the city was in danger.

"Hear that, lad? You had better get going. The city needs you." Mr. Wicked bowed slightly to Gabriel.

There was a loud crackling sound. Gabriel looked down at his wrist. The image of Mayor Dolan filled the tiny view screen. "Guardian? Are you there? We need your help."

Gabriel pressed the call switch and spoke. "I'm here, Mayor."

"Guardian. Thank goodness I've reached you in time. There are two atomic rockets headed toward downtown. We need you to stop them from destroying the city. I'm sending you their coordinates." The image of the mayor vanished, and a map of the city appeared with two flashing red blips moving fast from off shore.

"Don't worry, Mayor. I'm on it," Gabriel replied. Mr. Wicked was smiling from ear to ear. Gabriel felt flushed. "What should I do?" he asked Mr. Wicked.

"Why, fly, my boy. Fly fast and save the city!"

Gabriel wasn't certain that this was all real. For all he knew, this was just another one of Mr. Wicked's clever tricks. Gabriel peered over the edge of the building. He must have been at least fifty stories high. If he were the Eternal Guardian, then that would mean he could fly, but everything in his being told him that was impossible.

"What are you waiting for, Guardian?" Mr. Wicked asked. "You had better hurry or else hundreds of people will die."

"Listen, I'm not about to jump off this building. Do you hear me, pal?" Gabriel snapped back at Mr. Wicked. "Do you think I'm crazy?"

"You're not crazy, Gabriel. You're the Guardian." Mr. Wicked cast a coy gaze. "Here, you can do everything the Guardian can do. Even fly."

Again, the blaring roar of the Guardian's call echoed through the metropolis. "Guardian. We need your help. Please hurry," the mayor's panicked voice sparked out over Gabriel's wrist communicator as the missile blips moved faster toward shore. "Guardian. Please!"

A pair of silvery glints suddenly caught Gabriel's eye. They were little more than specs on the horizon, but Gabriel knew exactly what they were. It was up to him to stop those rockets. He had to believe in himself. He had to believe that he was the Guardian.

Gabriel closed his eyes, took a deep breath and leaped off the side of the skyscraper. I believe, he thought to himself. I am the Guardian. Gabriel could feel the wind blast past him, roaring through his ears as he fell. Fly, he thought. Fly. Gabriel opened his eyes. It was amazing! He wasn't falling as he first thought. He was indeed racing though the air at incredible speeds. Holding his hands out in front of him, he discovered that he was able to steer himself with ease.

"The missiles," he said aloud to himself. "I've got to stop them." Arcing a wide path in the air, he turned and raced out to sea. As he passed over the park, he could hear the crowds cheering and chanting his name. This feeling was awesome. He couldn't believe how fast he was moving, and before he knew it, he watched as the first of the two silver missiles blasted past him, filling his eyes with thick black smoke.

Gabriel turned in midair and raced after the first rocket. It was difficult to see because he was flying directly in the smoke trail that poured out of the hot exhaust port. He had no choice. If he couldn't see the missile, then he would have to feel for it. Racing closely behind the rocket, he reached out and felt for the missile's fins. The heat from the engine was terrific, and he was forced to turn his head away from the rocket's flame. Gabriel grasped about in the thick black smoke until his fingertips found the rocket's hot metal skin. Digging his fingers into the steel, he clutched the missile tightly. Rivets popped off and struck him in the face as the metal crumpled under his mighty grip.

Now that he had the rocket, he had to do something with it. Over his shoulder, he spotted the second missile following in the path of the first one. With a heave of his shoulder, he swung around, flinging the first rocket into the path of its twin. The two missiles collided, and the sky was filled with a fantastic explosion. The shockwave from the blast rippled out past the ocean and caused all of the windows in the nearby buildings to shatter. Far below him, the people all cheered. Some of the drivers honked their horns loudly in appreciation. Gabriel couldn't believe how great this felt. He had saved the day.

Flying gracefully back to Earth, Gabriel landed right on the steps of City Hall where the Mayor was waiting with his press entourage. "Thank you for saving us, Guardian. This city owes you a great debt," Mayor Dolan exclaimed while vigorously shaking Gabriel's hand.

"Anytime, Mayor," Gabriel replied smugly.

"Anytime, what?" Mr. Wicked replied coolly.

Gabriel felt dizzy and confused. He looked around and discovered that the world of the Guardian was now gone, and he was back in Mr. Silverman's living room. "You brought me back?" Gabriel asked.

"Of course I did. That was only a taste of what I have to offer you, and all you need to do is give your comic book to me. Give me Riley: Ace of the Skies, and everything you've ever wished can be yours."

Chapter Thirty:
THE DINNER FROM HELL

Gabriel's head was swimming. The sensation of actually being the Eternal Guardian was more than he was used to, and he still felt as if he could fly. Mr. Wicked stared at him from the other armchair, his silvery blue eyes twinkling.

"So, do we have a deal?" Mr. Wicked held out his right hand and waited for Gabriel to shake it.

Gabriel couldn't give up being the Eternal Guardian. It was too fantastic a feeling. Besides, it was just one comic book. What was that compared to being a superhero. Gabriel stood up. He lifted his right arm and held out his hand. Mr. Wicked began to smile. Anyway, it was really his dad's old book and what would he care? He was dead. Gabriel stopped and lowered his arm back down. My dad, Gabriel thought to himself. What would he do if he were here?

Mr. Wicked became flushed. "We have a deal now, don't we lad?" Mr. Wicked nodded and spread his long thin fingers toward Gabriel.

"Sorry, but I can't give up that comic book. It's the only thing I have left to remind me of my dad. Maybe I can trade you for a different one?"

Mr. Wicked's nostrils flared. "No. That's the comic book I want. And that's the comic book I'll get!" he snarled and crossed his arms. "It will only be a matter of time, Gabriel, but that comic book will be mine."

With a knock, Mr. Silverman popped his head into the living room. "Soup's on, guys. Come and get it while it's still hot."

Gabriel locked eyes with Mr. Wicked. He had never felt so uncomfortable in his life. He thought he should leave right away and skip dinner. Then Mr. Wicked did the unexpected, he smiled.

"Listen, Gabriel. I want to be your friend, and I want you to be my friend. We can help one another, you know. Work together. Be partners." Mr. Wicked stood and loomed over Gabriel. With a long, lanky arm he reached over and picked up the Eternal Guardian comic off the table. He placed it gently in Gabriel's hand. "Here. Take this as my gift. Think of it as a sign of my good faith, Gabriel." Mr. Wicked patted Gabriel on the shoulder. "My friend."

"Are you two coming or what?" Mr. Silverman grumbled.

Gabriel followed Mr. Silverman down the hallway toward the kitchen with Mr. Wicked bringing up the rear.

"I thought you had gotten lost. I was about to send out a search party," Mrs. Silverman joked as they entered the kitchen. Her oily, black beetle eyes fluttered their wings and scampered around to appear as if she were rolling her eyes at them. "Have a seat, Gabriel," she added, as she pulled out the center chair for him.

"Thank you." Gabriel choked. In the excitement of being the Guardian, Gabriel had forgotten about Mrs. Silverman's non-existent face and beetle eyes.

The rest of the group gathered around the table, and Mrs. Silverman walked over from the stove with a steaming hot casserole dish in her hands. She placed it in the center of the table. It smelled delicious.

"That smells wonderful, my dear. What culinary delight did you prepare for us tonight?" Mr. Wicked asked.

Mrs. Silverman reached out with a potholder and removed the lid to the casserole dish with a large flourish. "Why, I prepared Gabriel's favorite dish. Spaghetti and meatballs of course!"

Gabriel's mouth dropped open. The casserole dish was not filled with spaghetti and meatballs like Mrs. Silverman said. Instead, it was filled with globs of thick brown mud, filled to the brim with oozing, squirming earthworms.

"I made the sauce extra thick," Mrs. Silverman declared triumphantly. "Just the way growing boys like." Taking a large pair of salad tongs she scooped up a hearty helping of worms and mud and filled Gabriel's plate to the edge. She then did the same to Mr. Silverman and Mr. Wicked. Once the guests were served, she filled a plate for herself and sat down next to Gabriel. As Gabriel watched her fill the plates, he wondered how she was going to eat since she was missing a mouth. "Well, my handsome boys, dig in!"

Mr. Silverman took his fork and twirled up a large number of worms and mud then plopped the whole thing into his mouth as eagerly as if he were eating ice cream. "Um, delicious love. As always," Mr. Silverman declared with a mouth full of mud. Mrs. Silverman leaned over and mock kissed Mr. Silverman on the cheek. All the while, her beetle eyes stayed locked on Gabriel.

"How about you, honey? Aren't you hungry?" Mrs. Silverman asked Gabriel, cooing as if she were his own mother.

"I... uh," Gabriel tried to think fast. "I'm actually a little thirsty, that's all." Gabriel smiled meekly. The worms on his plate were beginning to free themselves from the mud and dangle over the edge of the table.

"Oh, my. Of course! Where are my manners?" Mrs. Silverman got up from her chair and took a clean glass out of the cupboard. She then went to the refrigerator and removed a plastic pitcher. Gabriel took the moment to steal a glace at Mr. Wicked. He was simply sitting there eating his worms and mud. With a giant slurp he sucked up an extra long worm and inhaled it with a pop. Gabriel felt like he was going to barf. Mrs. Silverman placed the clean glass in front of Gabriel and began filling it with some type of thick green sludge. It looked like pond scum. "What boy doesn't love a cool, refreshing glass of lemonade?" She laughed as she poured his glass full to the rim with the crusty green slime. Gabriel could swear one of her beetle eyes winked at him. He looked at the glass for a moment. He stomach was beginning to churn and do flips.

Pushing his chair straight back, Gabriel stood up like a shot. "I've got to go!" he shouted and dashed down the hallway. Grabbing his jacket from the hall closet, he bolted out the front door and made a mad grab for his bike. As he raced off into the night, he could hear Mr. Silverman calling after him. Gabriel wasn't sure exactly what Mr. Silverman was saying, but he swore it had something to do with dessert.

Chapter Thirty One:
INTO THE WOODS

Gabriel rode his bike as fast and as hard as he possibly could. His heart was pounding, and his lungs were burning. The chain of his bike rattled as he shifted gears and sped down the dark forest road. The only illumination came from the pale ring of light produced by the flashlight Gabriel had duct taped to his handlebars. It threw a soft cone of light onto the cracked asphalt road that led deeper and deeper into the woods. Eventually, the paved road turned to gravel and the gravel to dirt. As he pedaled down the dirt road, Gabriel soon found it nearly impossible to see where he was going due to all the dust his tires kicked up from the road. After a few moments, Gabriel slowed to a stop and rested one foot on the ground. Jumping off his bike, he let it fall to the road with a crash. He had made it. He was there, the old covered bridge deep in the heart of the forest.

"Hello?" Gabriel called out. "Vole? Are you there?" Gabriel peered into the ancient wooden bridge. In the dark of the night, it looked like someone had dropped a dilapidated old barn in the middle of the woods. He could see moonlight creeping through cracks in the roof and hear the trickle of creek water coming from beyond the floorboards beneath his feet. "Vole! It's me, Gabriel. I need your help!" he cried out.

Gabriel stood in the cool night air waiting for some sort of reply.

"Vole?"

Suddenly, something caught the corner of Gabriel's eye. It was walking slowly toward him from the far side of the bridge; a tiny creature no larger than a cat. But this was no cat. Gabriel recognized the shape in an instant. He had seen it many times before and it haunted the recesses of his mind so often that he was certain he would never forget it again. It was the fox. The same fox he had first spotted in the empty comic book store and the same fox that appeared on his windowsill during the storm.

Gabriel felt the cool night air against his sweaty brow as the animal drew closer. Then he spotted another one. The new fox was scurrying up through one of the broken planks in the floor. It clawed its way up and out where it simply sat and watched the first one continue to approach Gabriel. Then another fox appeared followed by another. During the time it took the original fox to cross the length of the bridge, at least twenty more foxes appeared. Some sat idly by while others scampered across the beams overhead and peered down at Gabriel with keen reflective eyes. Gabriel was surrounded. His breath quickened, and he had to fight every natural urge to turn and run. Finally, the original fox came to rest at Gabriel's feet.

For years after that evening, Gabriel found he was never able to properly describe what happened next because he had never seen anything like it before and has never seen anything like it since. In one swift fluid motion, the fox reared back on its hind legs and began to grow in size. Its arms lengthened and its nose shrank. The long bushy tail fell to pieces as the rest of its fur turned into a red sport coat and a pair of blue jeans. And after a moment, the fox was gone and all that remained was Vole.

"Hello, Gabriel. I'm glad you made it," Vole greeted Gabriel with a nod. Gabriel didn't reply. He simply stood there with a dumb look upon his face. "You may want to close your mouth before you let the bugs in," Vole added while tapping his lower lip.

"Bugs!" Gabriel exclaimed. "Mrs. Silverman's face-"

"Yes. Beetles for eyes. I know." Vole nodded. "I'm afraid that your teacher has become a pawn in a greater game. A game where the stakes may be your immortal soul."

"My soul?" Gabriel whispered.

"Yes. I'm afraid you may be in over your head, Gabriel. Didn't you get my message?"

"Message?"

"Yes. In the dirt. It took a great deal of work for me to craft that message for you. That's why it was so short. Beware the Devil. Remember?" Vole motioned with his finger as he wrote in the air. "I've been watching you closely from the moment he blew into town. In fact, I've been watching you closely ever since he first learned of your comic book."

"He? You mean Mr. Wicked?" Gabriel asked.

Vole chuckled to himself. "Yes. Mr. Wicked. Or whatever he fancies calling himself these days."

"I was just with him you know. I had dinner with him. They were trying to feed me worms for dinner."

Vole's eyes widened and he looked concerned, almost frightened. "You didn't eat any of their food I hope?"

"Yeah right, like I'm going to eat worms and mud." Gabriel rolled his eyes.

Vole took a deep breath and looked off into the forest. "I think it's high time I introduce you to someone, Gabriel. A person of great importance. Follow me." Vole walked over to the edge of the bridge and jumped down to the forest floor. Several foxes followed him.

Gabriel began to follow but hesitated for a moment. "What about my bike?"

"Don't worry," Vole called back. "My brothers and sisters will watch over it for you." Gabriel looked back to see the remaining foxes all sitting around his dirt bike. One was perched on the seat.

Taking a deep breath, Gabriel stepped off the path and followed Vole into the dark forest.

"Where are we going?" Gabriel asked. He was finding it difficult to keep up with Vole's long legs and even more difficult to see where he was going. Every so often he would run face first into a spider's web or catch a wiry tree branch smack in the cheek.

"You'll see. We must hurry. Time is precious now." Vole began to walk even faster, taking great strides over the forest floor. Now and then, Gabriel would glimpse another fox scampering alongside him or darting zig-zag through the underbrush.

"Who are we going to meet in here? We're pretty far into the woods. There's nothing out here. Is there?"

"Soon, all your questions will be answered. However, I'm afraid even newer and stranger questions may be raised," Vole replied with a half smile.

"You didn't answer my question," Gabriel grumbled. "I asked who are we-" but Gabriel was cut off in mid-sentence. He stopped cold in his tracks, causing one of the nearby foxes to crash into his sneakers.

Standing before him, bathed in the cool moonlight, were the ruins of old Foxfield. Everything here was broken and dilapidated. Enormous trees grew to dizzying heights. Some of them grew so large and wild that they cleaved whole buildings in two. Thick knotted tree limbs burst through the windows, and prickly tree roots wrenched the old plumbing out of the ground. Even the statue of the town founder, the Revolutionary War hero Jacob Smalls, was covered in thick green moss. So much so that his tri-corner hat was almost as round as a sombrero.

Suddenly, Gabriel heard something familiar. Something beautiful. It was singing. The same beautiful voice he had heard that night he had painted the fence. It was the voice that drew him into the forest in a trance. The singing was near, and it was clearer than it had ever sounded before. Gabriel found he was falling into the same trance all over again. "Who is that singing?" he asked in a daze.

"That is who we are going to visit." Vole smiled. "My mother, the Queen of the Foxes."

Chapter Thirty Two:
THE SECRET WAR OF THE FOXES

"Your mother?" Gabriel repeated. "Your mother is a queen?"

Vole didn't reply. He simply smiled and beckoned Gabriel to follow him. Together, the two walked through the forgotten streets of old Foxfield following the beautiful song. The remaining foxes trailing around Gabriel's feet quickly scampered off. Gabriel watched as the little foxes dashed ahead of them making a beeline toward the source of the singing.

As Gabriel and Vole turned the corner, Gabriel saw a bright light coming from the center of town. The light was so warm and so vivid that Gabriel thought it might be a bonfire. But it wasn't a bonfire. It wasn't anything of the sort. As Gabriel and Vole approached the old town square, Gabriel was astonished to find an enormous oak tree growing out of the middle of the central park fountain. The fountain, which had dried up years ago, was reduced to nothing more than a cracked marble planter for the enormous tree. A warm fire-like glow was coming from the base of the tree, as was the singing. The song was clearer now, and Gabriel listened to the words.

> *Riu, Riu, Chiu... la guarda ribera*
> *Dios guarde el lobo de nuestra cordera.*
> *Dios guarde el lobo de nuestra cordera.*

"Is that her?" Gabriel squinted through the dark in an effort to see better. "Is that your mother?" Again Vole didn't reply. He simply kept walking forward toward the tree. Gabriel followed.

Seated at the base of the tree was the most beautiful woman Gabriel had ever seen. She was slender and pale, with a crown of fiery red hair that washed down over her shoulders and back. She was draped in long ivory robes that seemed to disappear into the autumn leaves that covered the forest floor. In her arms she held a small baby who was also wrapped in similar ivory colored cloth. The woman possessed an ethereal glow that bathed the area around her in a warm soft light. She was surrounded by a multitude of bright orange foxes.

"Welcome, Gabriel Woods. I've been expecting you," the queen spoke in gentle tones that seemed to echo out through the forest.

"You have?" Gabriel walked closer.

"Indeed," she replied, gazing at Gabriel with her piercing green eyes. "I've been expecting you for a very long time. Since before you were born, actually."

Gabriel wasn't sure what to say or do. He glanced up to Vole who simply returned his puzzled gaze with a brief smile.

"Do not be alarmed, my young friend," the queen continued, "for I have existed in this world for a very long time. Longer than you could possibly imagine. I have waited a long time for this day. For you are destined to be of great assistance to my family and our ongoing war against the powers of darkness." The queen's words echoed out through the forest as she spoke, causing a sprinkling of leaves to fall from the canopy overhead.

"I don't get it. What do I have to do with anything?"

"I'm afraid you have everything to with us and our war." The queen smiled at Gabriel.

"What war?" Gabriel didn't like the sound of where this was all leading.

The queen took a moment and stroked her sleeping baby's head. "Our secret war against the Devil, of course. A war in which you will play an important part. For you see, many millennia ago, we foxes were simple creatures. We lived in the woods and in the hills. Our life was a peaceful life, full of blissful ignorance and innocence. However, for all of our simple ways, we had in our possession one precious gift. We were masters of disguise with the ability to blend into our surroundings and become invisible to both predator and prey. This precious gift allowed us to multiply and thrive in the wild.

"Then, one day, the Devil came to see my father and offered him a trade. He wished to trade the foxes for their uncanny ability to disguise themselves. In exchange, the Devil offered my father an unrivaled intellect that would make the foxes the smartest creatures in the forest. My father unwisely agreed to the deal. Unfortunately, I can not fault him, for at the time, we foxes were not the brightest of creatures." The queen nodded sadly to herself.

"What happened then?" Gabriel asked with keen interest.

"The Devil made good on his deal, of course," the queen replied. "However, when he took our ability to conceal ourselves, he also left us with quite another surprise. The Devil changed the beautiful brown of our fur coats to a blazing mix of orange and red, forever marking us with his colors and making us easy prey upon the dark forest floor. Soon our kind was hunted and eaten to near extinction. Our pelts were strung up like trophies and hunted for sport. It was then that we swore we would use our newfound intelligence to wage a war on the Devil. We will follow him to the end of the Earth, attempting to thwart his evil wherever he may venture."

"And that's why the foxes returned to Foxfield?" Gabriel remarked.

"Correct." The queen smiled.

"Does that mean that the Devil has been here before?"

The queen exchanged a knowing glance with Vole. "Perhaps. But that is not your story, Gabriel Woods. You are currently in the middle of quite a serious turn of events."

"So Mr. Wicked is the Devil," Gabriel said aloud to himself. "Man, this is getting weirder and weirder."

"Indeed."

"And he's after me?"

"He's after your comic book," Vole interjected. "Although I'm uncertain as to why. His actions often hide his true motives, and if you are not careful, he may take you as well, if you continue to get in his way."

"Take me?" Gabriel asked softly.

"Your soul," the queen replied. Gabriel's face began to grow white.

"You're frightening him, Mother." Vole placed a hand on Gabriel's shoulder. "It's not all that bad, Gabriel. There's more to this story than you know." Vole raised an eyebrow to the queen.

"I believe the Devil will not take your soul, Gabriel Woods," the queen continued, her words echoing through the treetops. "In fact, I have foreseen that you are destined to aid us in defeating him."

"You think I can beat the Devil?" The warble in Gabriel's voice betrayed his nervousness.

"You will not be able to defeat him permanently. Nevertheless, I have foreseen that you will be a great aid to us." The queen looked lovingly at the baby in her arms as she spoke. "I have no doubt you will succeed. It is your destiny. Vole will assist you."

"Of course." Vole smiled and nodded to Gabriel.

"He is my greatest student, and he will help you in your fight. He is one of the cleverest of my children, and he has relearned the ancient ability to transform and conceal himself in ways the Devil can not see." The queen then stood up to her full tremendous height and held out her hand toward Gabriel. "Come to me, Gabriel Woods." Gabriel didn't understand it, but he felt compelled to walk toward the queen. He stood before her and felt the warmth of her light. "Now kneel before me." Again, Gabriel felt as if he were still in a trance, and he bent down on one knee. The queen reached up and snapped a branch off the tree. "I knight thee, Sir Gabriel, defender of the faith, protector of all that is good and pure." She gently rested the leaves of the branch on

Gabriel's shoulder. Gabriel didn't understand it, but he was suddenly filled with a fantastic feeling. A feeling like he could do anything. A feeling as if he were invincible. The butterflies in his stomach were leaving. "Rise, sir knight, Order of the Foxes," the queen commanded. Gabriel stood back up. The queen then reached into her robe and removed a brown sphere which she handed to Gabriel.

"What's this?" Gabriel looked at the thing. It was a small round object made of clay about the size of a tangerine. Small holes were punched into its hollow flesh.

"It's an ocarina," Vole replied. Gabriel gave him a puzzled look. "It's like a clay whistle. Or flute," Vole explained.

"It is your weapon against evil," the queen added proudly. "For although we can not help you fight the Devil directly, we can aid you in thwarting the machinations of his design."

"Don't knights usually get swords?" Gabriel looked disappointedly at the ocarina.

"Your heart will be your sword. And love will be your shield," the queen replied. Gabriel became transfixed by her words as she stared at him with her piercing green eyes. "For you are about to journey into the heart of darkness, Gabriel Woods, and no sword on Earth would be able to protect you from what you must confront."

A distant sound of thunder rumbled from somewhere high overhead. Both Vole and the queen darted their heads skyward. Again, they exchanged a knowing glance. Several of the foxes sitting around the tree began to peel off and scurry back into the forest.

"Time for us to go, Gabriel," Vole said softly.

"But I have more questions… for the queen," Gabriel stammered as Vole began to leave.

"Another time maybe." Vole shook his head as he took Gabriel by the arm and hurried back toward the forest. Vole walked briskly as another blast of thunder shook the sky. In fact, he walked so fast with his long legs that he practically dragged Gabriel behind him. After a few moments, they left the ruins of old Foxfield and sped their way through the dark forest. Gabriel looked back over his shoulder and watched as the glow from the queen became dimmer and dimmer until nothing was left. Again, thunder shook the sky.

"Why are we leaving? Does it have something to do with the rain?" Gabriel asked as he tried to keep up with Vole's lengthy strides.

"That's not rain coming," Vole nervously replied as his eyes darted glances toward the sky. "That's him, Gabriel. He's searching for you."

Chapter Thirty Three:
MORTAL PERIL

The next morning, Gabriel woke early from bed and slipped downstairs as silently as possible. Reaching the pantry, he grabbed Grandpa Jerry's heating pad and brought it back upstairs to his room. Tucking it under the covers, he turned the knob to high and pressed it hard against his forehead.

"Rise and shine sleepyhead!" Mrs. Woods entered right on cue. "You'll have to tell me how dinner was. Did you talk to your teacher about bringing up your math grades?"

Gabriel rolled his eyes back into his head and let out a loud croak.

"Gabriel, are you alright?" Mrs Woods sat down on the bed next to Gabriel and placed her hand on his forehead. "Oh, honey. You're burning up. You must have a fever."

"Uh? Gooba. Wha?" Gabriel mumbled.

"You're not going to school today. You must have caught this from spending all that time out at night on your bike. It's not summer anymore you know." Walking into the hall closet, she soon returned with a bundle of blankets and placed the heap on Gabriel's bed. She then hurried downstairs and brought him two aspirins and a tall glass of water. "I need to get to work, but I'll try and come home early tonight to see how you're doing. Alright, honey?" Gabriel nodded weakly. Mrs. Woods kissed him on the forehead and closed the door gently as she left.

Gabriel waited silently in bed and listened as Mrs. Woods set up Grandpa Jerry's movie projector and then drove off down the road into town. A small orange fox darted onto Gabriel's windowsill and peeked inside. "Did it work?" Vole asked.

Gabriel wrestled himself free from the mountain of blankets and propped himself up against the wall. "Yeah, she fell for it. The coast is clear."

Vole jumped down off the windowsill and sat at the foot of Gabriel's bed.

"Why don't you transform?" Gabriel asked.

"Too risky. It's easier for me to hide if I stay in my natural form," the fox replied.

"Yeah. But it's weird talking to a fox," Gabriel replied as he got up and got dressed. Vole walked across Gabriel's bed and looked at the Eternal Guardian comic that Mr. Wicked had given Gabriel the previous night.

"I wonder why he's so interested in your comic book?" Vole asked aloud.

"Riley is a great comic." Gabriel shrugged. "Maybe he is just a collector. Like he said."

"Never trust the Devil, Gabriel," Vole said flatly. "There must be more to it."

"So you can change into anything? Like, can you transform into a chair? Or a hockey stick?" Gabriel asked as he tied his shoe.

"Almost anything. I can't become anything with moving parts. Like a watch for instance."

"That's why you asked me for the time that day, even though you were wearing a watch." Gabriel pointed to Vole. "Because you weren't wearing a watch at all. It was just part of your disguise."

"Exactly. Although I was actually asking you the time to see if you were alright or if he had gotten to you yet. I wasn't certain if you had received my note. That's also why Mr. Wicked thought I had broken into his store that day. He thought I was hiding somewhere in the shop disguised as a piece of furniture."

"So that's why he melted his own cash register? He thought it was you in disguise."

"Precisely."

Gabriel opened up a large cardboard box and began sorting through stacks of old comic books. "But if Mr. Wicked is the Devil, why didn't he just know I was hiding there? Why would he have been confused? Isn't he all knowing?"

Vole let out a hearty laugh. "Hardly!" He chuckled. "The Devil is not all knowing. Don't get me wrong. He's extremely powerful and dangerous, but he's not omnipotent. In fact, when he's in his mortal disguise, all of his powers become quite numb."

"His disguise? You mean Mr. Wicked. So, that's not what he looks like?"

"Heavens no. No one really knows what the Devil looks like. At least no one living knows."

"So what do we do? How do we beat him?"

"I have no idea." Vole shook his furry little head.

Gabriel stopped sorting comics and glared at Vole. "What? What do you mean you have no idea!"

"We'll figure something out." Vole shrugged. Gabriel was taken aback. He had never seen a talking fox shrug its shoulders before and he paused to absorb the strangeness of it all. Reaching into the box, he dumped a pile of comic books onto the bed.

"What are these for?" Vole asked.

"Research," Gabriel replied. "We're going to read every last one. Maybe we will get some idea of what Mr. Wicked is it up to and how to beat him."

Vole looked disapprovingly at the pile. "We have to read them all?"

"Yes."

Nudging the nearest book with his nose Vole tipped open the cover and began reading. It was an issue of the The Golden Glider: Intergalactic Defender of Justice.

"Vole," Gabriel spoke as he read.

"Yes?" Vole replied, as his eyes scanned the page.

"What was that acapella thing for?"

"You mean ocarina?"

Gabriel stopped reading. He reached into his coat pocket and removed the small clay whistle. "Yeah." Gabriel placed his lips to the largest hole and took a deep breath.

"Wait!" Vole shouted and instantly transformed into his human form. "Don't blow that whistle!" Vole snatched the ocarina from Gabriel's hand just as he exhaled a large puff of air. "This is an extremely old and powerful artifact. It's not a toy."

"What's so special about it?" Gabriel stared at the object.

Vole held the small clay flute very gently in his hands. "If you blow into it, the forest will come to your aide. But it is only to be used if you are in the utmost gravest of danger."

Gabriel looked nervously at the ocarina. "Vole?" Gabriel spoke slowly, "Am I going to be in the utmost gravest of danger?"

Vole looked at the tiny flute for a moment before answering. "I'm afraid that if my mother gave this to you, then yes, at some point your life will be in mortal peril."

Gabriel rested his head on his hand and glared at Vole. "Oh, that's just great."

Chapter Thirty Four:
ULTIMATUM

For the remainder of the day, Vole and Gabriel anxiously pored over almost every comic book in Gabriel's collection with little results. They created a series of piles with possible theories on Mr. Wicked's plans. Unfortunately, none of them were very concrete. Eventually, Vole bid Gabriel farewell and dashed off into the woods with a few of Gabriel's remaining comics clutched tightly in his tiny razor sharp teeth. Gabriel thought Vole should bring some comics to the queen to see if she could make anything out of them.

"You're looking better already," Mrs. Woods chimed in as she entered Gabriel's room and found him tucked neatly under the covers.

"I'm feeling a little better," Gabriel replied as he put down the comic he was reading and sat up in bed.

"I brought you some soup from the deli." Mrs. Woods rested a thick Styrofoam bowl and a plastic spoon down on the end table next to Gabriel.

Gabriel popped the top off the bowl and took a deep whiff of the steam that wafted up. "Ummm. Vegetable," he hummed. "Thanks, Mom."

Mrs. Woods clutched Gabriel by the top of his head and scrambled his hair. "No problem, kiddo."

"Mom!" Gabriel protested as he smoothed out his hair the best could.

"Did Grandpa Jerry check in on you at all?" Mrs. Woods asked as she stood up and slung her green work apron over her shoulder.

"No," Gabriel mumbled with a mouth full of hot soup.

"That's funny. I asked him to stop by and see you today," Mrs. Woods replied as she walked over to the window and slid it closed. "You should really keep this window shut if you're not feeling well, honey. This night air isn't good for you."

"I'm feeling better now." Gabriel slurped more soup.

"Yeah. Which reminds me. There's something we need to talk about." Gabriel recognized the change in Mrs. Woods voice. She spoke in that type of voice that you knew wasn't going to be good news. "I know it's only a day away, but I think you may need to skip going out on Halloween this year."

Gabriel stopped eating his soup. "What? Why?"

"Because you're sick, that's why. This has been a very strange month and I don't think you should tempt fate any more by going out in the cold night air, especially if you are getting over a flu." Mrs. Woods put her hands on her hips and cocked her head in a way that said, don't mess with me. Gabriel opened his mouth to protest, but seeing the signs, figured this was one battle he wasn't going to win. "Now finish your soup. I'll be back in a minute with a fresh glass of water and some more aspirin. But first, I'm going to go say hi to Grandpa Jerry."

"But Mom! The candy!" Gabriel cried. Mrs. Woods wasn't taken in and simply winked at Gabriel as she left the room.

Gabriel continued to eat his dinner and stare out the window. It seemed to be getting darker earlier and earlier, and all he could see now was his own reflection staring back at him from the glass.

"Good evening, Gabriel," a man spoke in cool tones from somewhere behind him. Gabriel jumped out of his skin, spilling his soup all over his blanket. Whipping around, he was shocked to discover Mr. Wicked standing in the darkest corner of his room.

"What!" Gabriel declared. "What are you doing here? How did you get in my room?"

"You let me in, Gabriel," Mr. Wicked calmly replied through his crooked smile. "Little bright in here, isn't it?" Mr. Wicked asked as he walked up to the lamp in the corner and blew out the bulb as easily as if he were snuffing out a candle. Gabriel sat in the darkness listening to his own heart beat. With his lamp extinguished, the only source of illumination now came from the dim yellow glow of the hallway light. "Ah, that's better. Nice and cozy."

Gabriel edged back. Sitting there in his pajamas, he had never felt more vulnerable or afraid in his entire life. "What do you want?"

"Oh, Gabriel. All I've ever wanted is to be your friend." Mr. Wicked continued to creep closer. "But you don't seem very interested in being my friend." Mr. Wicked shook his head sadly. "I introduced you to my family, showed you a magnificent world few have ever seen, and even gave you a rare and wonderful gift."

"What gift?" Gabriel was flustered. He needed to think of something and fast. He couldn't have his mother come back up and find Mr. Wicked there.

"The Eternal Guardian comic, of course." Mr. Wicked was so close now that Gabriel could see into his eyes. The silvery blue twinkle had vanished and was now replaced with an unnerving red haze like you get when you take bad snapshots. "And how do you repay my kindness, Gabriel? By going in league with those filthy forest rodents!" Mr. Wicked's voice grew louder as he grinded the word rodents through his back teeth.

Gabriel was starting to panic. He felt large beads of sweat roll down the back of his neck. He needed to get out of there. But where could he run? The Devil could be anywhere. He had to figure out a way to get rid of Mr. Wicked.

"But I digress." Mr. Wicked's voice returned to the cool collected tones Gabriel had become accustomed to. "I'm here to offer you one last chance, Gabriel."

"One last chance?" Gabriel repeated.

"Yes." Mr. Wicked nodded solemnly. "You must bring your Riley: Ace of the Skies comic book to my shop by midnight tomorrow night and willingly give it to me as a gift."

How could Gabriel get rid of Mr. Wicked? His mind raced. What did Mr. Wicked mean when he said Gabriel had let him in? How did he let him in?

"What if I refuse?" Gabriel replied, stalling for time.

"If you refuse, then I can't be responsible for what happens to your lovely mother." Mr. Wicked shrugged.

Gabriel felt his stomach drop. "What do you mean by that?" he demanded. Mr. Wicked didn't reply. He simply continued to smile a steely cold smile. "Tell me!" Gabriel shouted.

Suddenly, a blood curdling scream shook the house. Gabriel leapt out of bed and grabbed the baseball bat resting on the floor by his closet. "Mom!" he yelled. "Mom are you alright?"

"It's all up to you now, Gabriel." Mr. Wicked grinned. "Only you can save her. Bring me the comic book and all will be right. Refuse me, and she dies." With that, Mr. Wicked took a deep breath and blew out all the lights in the house with a single puff. Gabriel listened to his own heart pounding as the room was plunged into complete and total darkness.

Chapter Thirty Five:
AN OLD FRIEND

"Mom!" Gabriel cried out again.

No reply.

"It's too late for her, Gabriel," Mr. Wicked smiled a cruel smile, "but not for you."

Gabriel edged himself closer to the doorway and peered out into the hall. It was pitch black inside the old farmhouse. Gabriel frantically flipped the light switch, but nothing happened. "Mom! Are you alright?" he shouted again. Again, there was no reply.

Gabriel clutched the baseball bat so tightly that pools of sweat poured down the wooden shaft. Suddenly, a crashing noise thundered through the house. It sounded as if someone had tipped over a bookcase full of anvils. Gabriel slowly ventured into the hallway and crept silently towards the top of the wooden staircase. His eyes were slowly adjusting to the darkness, and he was able to make out the edges of the steps in the moonlight.

Then, for an instant, he thought he had spotted something. A large lumbering shape twisting its way past the staircase. A strange guttural raspy noise followed in the object's wake.

"I wouldn't go down there if I were you," Mr. Wicked taunted Gabriel from the edge of his bedroom. Looking back, Gabriel didn't understand why Mr. Wicked didn't follow him into the hall. He simply stood just inside the bedroom glaring back out at Gabriel. Gabriel returned the dirty look and slowly began descending the staircase.

"Mom? Grandpa Jerry?" Gabriel called out. Then another crashing noise echoed up from the darkness, followed by long raspy breaths. Each plank creaked and moaned as Gabriel tiptoed barefoot down the cold wooden steps. Reaching the bottom of the stairs Gabriel peered into the darkness and scanned the room for any sign of his mother.

All he could see was that something had completely crushed the raggedy old dining room table, fracturing it into a puzzle of broken wood and splinters. Most of the chairs had also been destroyed. One of the old chair legs had been thrown clear through the television screen. Gabriel squeezed the bat even tighter now, almost to the point of cutting off the circulation to his fingers. Again, he heard the raspy breathing sound. This time it was coming from the kitchen.

Gabriel began inching toward the kitchen door. His eyes kept darting up and back from the floor to the door. He had to be sure not to step on any splinters or broken glass in his bare feet. Turning the corner, Gabriel leaned over to see if he could peek into the kitchen without actually going into it. Stretching out with all of his might, Gabriel craned his neck and peered into the room.

Everything had been destroyed. The refrigerator was ripped out of the wall and tossed open onto its side. The remaining bits of leftovers and condiments had exploded all over the walls and the floor. The cabinet doors were all flung open and broken. Shattered dishes were strewn upon the floor and peppered with countless bent utensils. And laying in a crumpled ball in the center of the room was Gabriel's mother.

"Mom!" Gabriel shouted and raced over to her side. Lifting her head, Gabriel shook her shoulders and hugged her tightly. "Mom! Mom! Please wake up!" Mrs. Woods lay limp as a rag doll in Gabriel's young arms.

"Gaaabbbrielll.." a dark voice hissed, "Isss that you?" Gabriel heard the voice coming from somewhere behind him. "Gaaaabbbbrielll, I've missssssed you."

Gabriel stood up and held the bat out at arm's length. Standing before him was a colossal monster. It looked like an enormous snake except that it had two large powerful arms that it used to drag itself around, and in place of eyes, were two gigantic black beetles that fluttered and scurried around the serpent's face. "Mrs. Silverman?" Gabriel gasped.

"Yoooou remember meeeeee," the creature growled. "Cooome back wiiiith meeeeee." Mrs. Silverman swung her leathery tail across the room sending the couch tumbling.

"Don't come near her! You hear me! Don't you dare hurt my mother!" Gabriel demanded through a quivering voice.

"I'll beeeeee your mothhhher now, Gaaabbbriellllll," Mrs. Silverman hissed and flashed her beetle eyes at him. "Now, cooome with meeeee." The enormous serpent lunged at Gabriel with her powerful arm. Gabriel darted past the beast and slid back into the living room.

Mrs. Silverman sprung around and dove after Gabriel, missing him by inches. Gabriel swung the bat as hard as he could, striking the monster on its claw. Mrs. Silverman let out a shriek. Gabriel raced as fast as he could back up the staircase. Tripping on the steps, he stumbled, and the baseball bat slipped through his sweaty fingers. Turning after it, Gabriel spied Mrs. Silverman thundering across the living room floor after him.

"Oh man! Oh man! Oh man!" Gabriel stammered as he left the bat behind and scrambled up the flight of stairs as fast as his legs would carry him. The stairwell was a narrow fit for the enormous serpent, and Mrs. Silverman quickly became jammed in the hallway. With one last lightning fast movement, the monster lunged out after Gabriel catching him by the back of his pajama top. Gabriel wriggled like mad and freed himself just as the creature tore the shirt from his body. Diving back into his bedroom, Gabriel tumbled past Mr. Wicked who was still waiting by the doorway.

"I told you not to go down there," Mr. Wicked pouted and shook his head.

Gabriel stumbled to his feet and looked back at the door. He could hear Mrs. Silverman thrashing about in the stairwell struggling to squeeze through and get him. Gabriel's mind raced. "What do I do?" he asked aloud.

"Give up, silly boy," Mr. Wicked chuckled. "You're way out of your league." Checking the hallway, he frowned and looked back at Gabriel. "You had better hurry. She's almost here." Mr. Wicked frowned. "And she looks rather upset."

Gabriel tried to calm down. He needed to think of what to do. What would Vole do in his place, he thought to himself. "Vole!" he exclaimed as he realized what he needed to do. Dashing over to his jacket, he dug into the pocket and removed the ocarina.

"Where did you get that?" Mr. Wicked shrieked, and for the first time ever, Gabriel heard the sound of fear in Mr. Wicked's voice. Gabriel didn't answer. Mrs. Silverman was already snaking her long head into his room.

"Gaaabbbbbrielllll. Come toooo meeeee!" Mrs. Silverman snarled as she began to claw away at the doorframe.

Gabriel raced over to the window and threw it open. He took a deep breath of crisp autumn air and held it for just a moment as he leaned out the open window. Then, placing the ocarina to his lips, he blew into the small sphere as hard as he possibly could!

An extremely high pitched tone sang out from within the tiny clay whistle. Mrs. Silverman froze in her tracks. Mr. Wicked looked dumbfounded. Gabriel watched as the sound blasted its way through the forest cleaving tree-tops and leaving an explosion of leaves in its wake. Then all was silent. All was still. There was no murmur of wind. No chirp of crickets. Nothing. An eerie calm fell over the farmhouse, like a ship passing though the eye of a hurricane.

"Gaaabbbbrielllll. You willlll cooome with meeeeee now!" Mrs. Silverman ordered as her beetle eyes glared at Gabriel. "Or elssssse."

"It's over, Gabriel," Mr. Wicked cooed. "No one can help you now."

Gabriel felt strange. It must have had something to do with the ocarina because he was suddenly filled with a feeling of strength and power. It was the same feeling he had when the queen knighted him.

Suddenly, the air was broken by what sounded like the tone from the ocarina echoing back from somewhere deep within the heart of the forest. Out the window, Gabriel watched as a great wave washed across the canopy of tree-tops. It was as if the entire forest was bending in unison, sending an enormous wash of trees and leaves toward the farmhouse. Gabriel didn't look away, and he dared not blink for fear of missing the tremendous sight to come.

Chapter Thirty Six:
ONE WAY OUT

Out of the forest poured an ocean of scarlet and orange. A great wave of foxes rushed out from trees and crashed down upon the tiny farmhouse. Hundreds of foxes circled the house and began scampering up the sides until they started pouring in through Gabriel's bedroom window like a tidal wave. In an instant, the multitude of foxes washed over Mrs. Silverman, sending the beetle eyed creature tumbling back down the stairs.

"Ssssstop! You veeerrmmmminn!" the creature hissed and scowled as it crashed to the floor below.

Mr. Wicked didn't flinch. He simply stood to one side and watched the flood of foxes pour through the window and down the stairs.

"Gabriel! Be careful!" Vole called out as the tiny black footed fox leapt in through the window and transformed back into his human shape before hitting the floor.

"Vole! My you're looking a bit more ragged for wear," Mr. Wicked snarled.

"Gabriel, how did he get in here?" Vole bent down and grabbed Gabriel by the shoulder.

"I don't know." Gabriel shook his head. "He just showed up." Downstairs, the commotion grew louder. Every so often, Gabriel could hear the squeal of a fox in pain or the roar of Mrs. Silverman.

"It's been a long time, Vole." Mr. Wicked continued. "How is your dear mother doing? You know she isn't long for this world, don't you?" Vole glared back at Mr. Wicked. "Oh, you didn't know that? Well, I'm sorry to be the bearer of bad tidings. However, no one lives forever."

Vole picked up the nearby lamp and threw it at Mr. Wicked. The lamp passed clear through his body as if he were nothing more than a ghost. "Gabriel!" Vole looked deep into Gabriel's eyes. "Tell me. Has he left this room?" Vole pointed to Mr. Wicked.

"No," Gabriel stammered. "It's my mom. She needs my help. That monster downstairs is Mrs. Silverman!"

"I know." Vole tried to calm Gabriel's frantic tone.

"No. Vole, listen to me! My mother... My mother is-"

"Dead?" Mr. Wicked interjected. Vole rose up to his full lanky height, walked right up to Mr. Wicked's face. "Do you think you can intimidate me, rodent?" Mr. Wicked growled. "I've been around since the dawn of time, and I'll be around long after you have passed on."

"Gabriel. Where is that comic book he gave you?" Vole asked calmly, all the while never breaking eye contact with Mr. Wicked.

Gabriel raced over to his jacket pocket and removed the Eternal Guardian comic book. "Here it is." He waved the book at the back of Vole's head.

"Destroy it!" Vole ordered. Another monstrous crashing sound shook the house. Several foxes were scampering back up the steps licking their wounds.

"What?" Gabriel asked, looking at the comic as if it were the last one on Earth.

"Do it now!" Vole shouted. Gabriel slid the comic from the bag and held it at arm's length. Mr. Wicked flinched only for a moment as Gabriel ripped the comic book in two. As he did the book burst into flames and disappeared altogether before hitting the floor. Mr. Wicked returned Vole's glare as he began to grow transparent.

"Bravo," Mr. Wicked spat as he vanished from sight.

Vole's shoulders dropped. He spun around and smiled weakly to Gabriel. "One down," he said.

"Vole. It's my mom. I need to get her out of here," Gabriel gasped as he put his jacket on.

"Come on," Vole gestured as he sprung down the staircase with Gabriel in tow.

The living room was almost completely destroyed. A sea of scarlet foxes (both living and dead) covered the floor. In the center of the room, the monstrous form of Mrs. Silverman flung her powerful arms as she attempted to swipe at the legions of foxes clawing and biting her leathery skin. Vole took Gabriel by the hand and led him through the fight. "Your mother. Where is she?" Vole asked.

"In the kitchen." Tears started to well up in Gabriel's eyes. "What if Mr. Wicked is right? What if she's-"

"Don't say it." Vole cut him off as the two worked their way through the living room to the kitchen.

"There." Gabriel pointed to Mrs. Woods who was still laying on the floor.

"Gaaaabbbriiellll!" Mrs. Silverman shrieked. "Whhhyyy are yooouuu doooing thissssss toooo meeeee?" The creature was enraged and began tossing foxes violently across the room as it lumbered toward Gabriel.

"Hurry up now, Gabriel," Vole said as he pushed Gabriel across the kitchen floor. "We need to get her out the back way." Vole picked up Mrs. Woods and dragged her toward the back door of the kitchen. Mrs. Silverman was right behind them. Vole pushed on the tattered screen door.

Wham!

The door struck the spruce tree that marked the edge of the forest. The opening was too narrow for Vole to get through.

"Yoooouuuuuu!" Mrs. Silverman rolled a beetle eye toward Vole. "Yoo-ouuuuuu! Sssssstop!"

With one great heave, Vole slipped Gabriel's mother through the narrow gap of the door. "You're next, Gabriel."

"No. I can't leave you, too!" Gabriel shouted.

"I'll be right behind you, Gabriel." Vole winked. "I'm a fox, remember." Gabriel nodded and squeezed himself through the opening in the door. The night air was brisk, and the grass was covered with a freezing cold layer of wet dew. "Get your mother to safety," Vole said as Gabriel watched him close the door. "I have unfinished business to attend to." Gabriel raced back towards the opening, but he was too late. The last thing he could see was the gigantic form of Mrs. Silverman rearing up behind Vole as he closed the door and locked it with a click.

Chapter Thirty Seven:
GABRIEL WOODS' WILD RIDE

The sounds of the fight raged on inside the house. Gabriel tried desperately to open the back door, but it was locked tight. "I have to trust Vole. I have to trust Vole." He repeated to himself. "I need to be part of the solution, not the problem," he added looking down at his unconscious mother.

Running around the side of the house, Gabriel grabbed the overturned wheelbarrow from beside the shed and slid his mother onto its dirt encrusted scoop. Lifting with all of his might, he struggled with the wobbly wheelbarrow until he reached the garage door. Above him, the gigantic monstrous form of Mrs. Silverman crashed into the front porch windows shattering them all over the front lawn. Broken shards of glass rained down on Gabriel as he opened the garage door with a heave.

"Grandpa Jerry?" Gabriel called out into the dark garage. "Grandpa?" Gabriel flicked the light switch but, like the rest of the house, the power was still out.

Gabriel rolled the wheelbarrow deep into the dark garage until he banged into something. It was Grandpa Jerry's Studebaker! Opening the door, he piled his mother into the back seat and wrapped the seatbelt around her tightly. Gabriel then closed the door and jumped into the driver's seat where he found a surprise. Grandpa Jerry was sleeping in his pajamas and robe across the front seat. "Grandpa! Wake up! Wake up!" Gabriel shook Grandpa Jerry's shoulders.

"Wha? What is it?" Grandpa Jerry snorted himself awake. "Where's my movie? Where's Jack Lemmon? What happened to my projector?" he demanded.

"Grandpa. It's Mom! She's been attacked by... something. I think she's hurt." Gabriel gestured to the back seat.

"Gloria?" Grandpa Jerry peeked over the high back seat. "Glory? Are you alright, sweetie?"

At first, Gabriel hadn't noticed how quiet it had become. The crashing and noises seemed to have stopped, and he found the silence to be infinitely more unsettling than all the commotion and din. Was Vole alright? Was the battle over? A long shadow fell across the car as the moonlight that had been pouring in through the garage door was suddenly snuffed out. Peering through the windshield Gabriel saw the ominous silhouetted form of Mrs. Silverman creeping in through the garage door. Her large, oily black beetle eyes glistened in the silvery moonlight.

"Buckle up!" Gabriel shouted as he turned the ignition and started the car.

"What in Eisenhower's name are you doing, boy?" Grandpa Jerry spouted as the headlights turned on and Gabriel hit the gas. The old car, which hadn't been moved in ages, suddenly remembered what it meant to be alive and roared to life. Gabriel floored it and the jalopy thundered out of the garage and sped past Mrs. Silverman's hulking arms. The car shook and bucked as it rumbled over the rocks and branches, sending Grandpa Jerry crashing to the floor.

A bright white light flared up within the rear view mirror. At first, Gabriel thought there was another car behind them but seeing that he was still trampling over the wild cucumbers that dotted his lawn, he quickly thought otherwise. The light was tremendous, and Gabriel found that he had to squint hard just to see through the glare. In the middle of the flaring glow, Gabriel thought, just for a moment, he spotted the Queen of the Foxes standing in his living room. Then, as quickly as it had appeared, the light was gone.

Crashing into the street, Gabriel overcompensated as he attempted to drive the car down the forest road. "Gabriel! Stop this car at once!" Grandpa Jerry ordered and Gabriel let his foot off the gas. The car slowed down and eventually stopped. "What's gotten into you, boy?" Grandpa Jerry asked wide eyed as he picked himself up off the floor.

"We need to get her to a hospital!" Gabriel began to cry. Tears were starting to stream down his face. "We need to get her somewhere safe." Gabriel reached over and hugged his Grandpa.

Grandpa Jerry returned the embrace. He looked at his daughter who was slumped over the back seat still unconscious. "All right, Gabriel," he said softly. "Move over. I'll drive."

Chapter Thirty Eight:
THE HOSPITAL

Gabriel sat on the examination table. He wore a paper gown that was itchy and uncomfortable. His feet dangled off the edge where they swung about freely, as the nurse finished wrapping thick white bandages around his toes. He hadn't noticed it at the time, but he had apparently cut his bare feet in several places getting his mother out of the house.

"There you go," the nurse said as she snipped off the remaining stub of tape. "You were lucky you didn't need any stitches."

"Yeah, lucky I guess," Gabriel mumbled.

"Just one thing left now," she continued as she walked over to the galvanized silver tray and removed a small syringe. "Doctor says you should get a booster tetanus shot. Just to be safe." She winked at Gabriel. "Now this should only hurt for a moment." Swabbing Gabriel's skin, she plunged the shot into his arm.

"Ouch!" Gabriel yelped. "I thought you said I was lucky."

Gabriel's pajama bottoms were so dirty and torn from escaping the house that the hospital gave him a new set of light blue hospital scrubs to wear home.

The hospital waiting room was a bleak and sterile place. The green fluorescent lights flooded the chamber with a pale uncomfortable light. Old discarded magazines dotted the chairs and an annoying humming noise emanated from a small, half full water cooler resting in the corner. The only person in the room was Grandpa Jerry who smiled to Gabriel as he entered the room.

"How are your feet?" Grandpa Jerry asked, looking at Gabriel's bandages.

"Not half as sore as my arm," Gabriel replied rubbing his shoulder.

"How's Mom doing?"

Grandpa Jerry smiled a weak smile and sat back down on the bench. "She's still unconscious. Doctor says she may have a concussion. They're going to do some more tests." Grandpa Jerry nodded solemnly as he spoke.

"When is she going to wake up?" Gabriel asked.

Grandpa Jerry frowned. Gabriel always remembered that even though his grandpa's eyes welled up with tears, he never cried. "They don't know," he finally said. "Maybe tonight. Maybe never."

Gabriel didn't know what to say. All he could muster was, "I wish Dad was here."

Grandpa Jerry put his arm around Gabriel and hugged him tight. "Me too, kid. Me too."

Chapter Thirty Nine
WEEDS AND VINES

Gabriel and Grandpa Jerry spent the remainder of the night in the hospital. Eventually, the doctors suggested that they go home to get some rest and change clothes.

Grandpa Jerry parked his car in front of the house instead of in the garage. He had decided that he would take a quick shower and go back to the hospital to wait.

Gabriel opened the door to a disaster zone. Everything in the house was smashed. It looked as if the sofa had exploded. The foam from the cushions blanketed the floor along with more fractured planks of splintered wood and glass. "What on Earth could have done this?" Grandpa Jerry asked as he entered the farmhouse.

Although Gabriel knew the answer to that question, he stayed silent. What had happened to all the foxes? He knew many of them couldn't have survived that battle, but there was no sign of them. Not one red hair remained. "I don't know. It was dark, and the power was out. Do you think we were broken into by thieves?" Gabriel tried his best to sound as surprised as Grandpa Jerry.

Bending over the shredded remains of the couch, Grandpa Jerry picked at the torn fabric. "I don't think this mess was man-made. Maybe an animal? A bear ya think?"

"Looks like it could have been a bear. I guess we'll never know for sure." Gabriel shrugged and tried to sound as confused as his grandfather.

Grandpa Jerry threw a skeptical look at Gabriel. "Right," he finally replied. "I guess we'll never know." Grandpa Jerry stopped picking at the couch and pointed to the center of the floor. "What do you make of that?" Gabriel walked over to the middle of the room and squatted down for a closer look. Thick weeds and vines were growing out from in between the floor boards and the end table was growing a thick coat of fresh moss. "And that!" Grandpa Jerry pointed to the old wooden clock hanging on the wall. Gabriel looked up and couldn't believe his eyes. There appeared to be a new, tiny tree limb growing out of the side of the clock. A delicate spray of white flowers sprang from the tip.

"I have no idea," Gabriel muttered.

"Look at the time!" Grandpa Jerry shouted as his eyes roamed from the little branch to the clock's face. "I gotta get cleaned up."

About an hour later, Grandpa Jerry was showered and dressed in his old tweed suit. "Stay here," he told Gabriel. "I'm going back to the hospital. I'll call you if there's any change in your mother. In the meantime, I want you to start cleaning this mess up. Your mother will kill us both if she sees the house like this. Got me?"

"Gotcha," Gabriel replied.

"I'll be back later tonight. Stay out of trouble," he added, as he closed the door behind him. Gabriel waited patiently and watched until Grandpa Jerry's car was completely gone from sight. He then ran upstairs, put on a fresh pair of blue jeans and a tee shirt, grabbed his bike, and rode off into the woods toward the old covered bridge.

Chapter Forty:
BEATING THE DEVIL

"Vole! Vole, are you there?" Gabriel called out into the old covered bridge. It was the middle of the afternoon, and in the daytime, the bridge didn't seem nearly as frightening as it had the other night. In fact, with the birds chirping and the murmuring brook below, it was actually pretty pleasant.

"Gabriel?" Vole replied.

"Vole, where are you?" Gabriel asked, craning his neck to see into the rafters.

"Down here," Vole called out. Gabriel walked over to the edge of the bridge and looked down toward the creek. Vole was laying on his back with his feet in the water. He was in his human form, but all of his clothes were dirty and torn. His hair was a mess and he had not only a black eye, but a large cut on his cheek. All in all, he looked terrible.

Gabriel leapt over the railing and landed next to Vole with a muddy splash. "Are you okay? How badly are you hurt?"

Vole laughed then coughed. "Oh, I'll live." He smiled. "I just need a little rest, that's all."

"Should we get you to a doctor?"

"No. I can't go to a human doctor. They would see right through my disguise."

"Do you want me to take you to a vet?" Gabriel felt helpless. His entire world was crumbling down around him. First, his favorite place on Earth was taken away from him, then his mother, and now, his new best friend.

"That's a sweet thought, but no... thank you," Vole added. "Rest is all I need. We had a terrible time defeating that creature."

"Is Mrs. Silverman dead, then?" Gabriel asked.

Again, Vole laughed then coughed. "Dead? Well, let's just say she won't be back."

"That's not an answer," Gabriel groaned.

"Fortunately, for all of us, my mother arrived in the nick of time. She was able to dispatch that beast. You may have seen her. She was entering the house when you sped away in that car." Vole rubbed his swollen eye.

"Was that the glow I saw? The queen?" Gabriel asked.

"Yes. That was her. However, I don't think your house will ever be the same again," Vole replied then coughed. "I'm afraid I won't be of much help protecting you for a little while, Gabriel." Vole shook his head. "I need to rest." He closed his eyes and laid his head down on the cool muddy bank.

Gabriel sat down on the dry part of the creek bed. "I don't know what to do, Vole. I have to bring Mr. Wicked my comic book by midnight or else he'll kill my mom."

"So, what are you going to do?" Vole asked with his eyes still closed.

"Give in, I guess. It's just a dumb old book. If I had sold it years ago like mom wanted, then none of this would be happening now!" Gabriel's voice grew louder as he spoke, and he punctuated the moment by flinging a rock into the water.

"You can't live in the past. There's no point," Vole replied. "What's done is done. You can give in to him if you think that is best, but you will never be certain that his power is broken over you or your mother. The only way to be certain is to best him."

"You're the fox. Can't you come up with a clever idea?" Gabriel was fuming. He didn't mean to take out his frustration on his friend, but he was at the end of his rope. "I mean come on, how can I beat the Devil?"

"Beat the Devil? What sort of nonsense are ya spouting boy?" a crusty old voice called to Gabriel from the bridge. Gabriel looked up to see Ahab the trapper gazing down at him.

"Ahab? What are you doing here?" Gabriel leapt to his feet. Ahab walked with a slow lumbering limp over to the edge of the creek bed.

"Checking my traps for the little red devils," he replied and rattled a rusty pair of metal jaws in Gabriel's face.

"Have you caught any foxes yet, Mr. McCartney?" Vole called out from the ground.

Ahab scrunched his face and glared at Vole. "Not yet. But I will. Ya have me word on it. I will catch the rascals."

"I'm sure you will. They are only dumb animals after all," Vole calmly replied, his eyes still shut tight.

"Yer darn right, I will. Ye'll see," Ahab grumbled through his thick Cape Cod accent. "Now, what's all this about the Devil, boy?" Ahab cast his gaze upon Gabriel.

Gabriel looked to Vole for some type of excuse not to explain things to Ahab, but he just lay there with his eyes closed cooling his feet in the water. "Well you see, Mr. Ahab, I uh... I... well... there's this guy... In school, and he keeps getting the better of me. He's too clever for me to beat. And I don't know what to do about it." Gabriel stumbled over his own words as he tried to make up a plausible excuse.

Ahab simply stared at Gabriel with the type of look often reserved for crazy people. "So, there's this guy?"

"Right."

"And he's too clever fer ya?"

"Right."

"Cagey like the Devil, ya say?" Ahab rubbed his thick stubble with a leathery hand.

"Yeah. Like the Devil." Gabriel added. "How can I beat a guy like that?"

A good minute passed as Ahab stood and thought about Gabriel's question. "Well," he finally began. "My father used to say, if yer gonna fight the Devil, then yer gonna have to be a devil yerself."

"What the heck does that mean?" Gabriel threw up his arms exasperatedly.

"It means use your enemy's strengths against him," Vole chimed in.

"Right," Ahab replied. "Fight fire with fire. Hellfire!" Ahab began laughing, and surprisingly, Vole joined him.

"What are you two laughing about?" Gabriel shook his head in frustration. "How can I use his own power against him. I don't have any power to..." Gabriel's voice began to trail off as he thought about the problem. "Wait a minute. That's it!" Gabriel raised a muddy finger. "Vole! I think I know what we have to do." Gabriel scrambled across the creek bed and whispered in Vole's ear. "Can you meet me tonight at my house? I'm going to need your help."

"I don't know if I can be much help to you, Gabriel." Vole finally opened his eyes and propped himself up in the mud.

"You don't have to do much. But it's something only you can do."

Ahab looked back and forth at Gabriel and Vole. "What're ya two devils scheming about now?"

Vole and Gabriel looked at one another, then turned in unison to Ahab. "Nothing." They both shrugged at the same time.

"Right." Ahab scowled. "Then why are the two of ya wearing such devilish grins?"

Chapter Forty One:
HALLOWEEN

Gabriel sat on his bike and waited on the outskirts of town. Slung over his shoulder was an old bed sheet with a pair of eye holes cut out of the center. It was supposed to be a ghost costume, but he had no intentions of wearing the thing. He kept the makeshift costume close by just in case someone walked past and spotted him out on Halloween alone.

Down in the center of town, he could see the tiny shapes of the other children all trick-or-treating with their parents. It was only seven o'clock, but the sun had already been down for a good hour. Gabriel watched as the little ghouls and goblins passed in and out of the pale glow of the streetlights. Gabriel wasn't interested in trick-or-treating tonight. He had a different plan in mind for this special evening, and he kept his sights on the tiny brick building on the edge of town. It was the store in which he had spent most of his childhood, and he was about to take it back. Wicked Books.

"Hello, Gabriel." Vole scampered up from the shadows in his fox form and perched himself on the hood of a parked car.

"Is everything set?" Gabriel asked.

"I don't know if this is such a good idea, Gabriel. It's a risky plan," Vole replied. "Don't underestimate him."

"I bet he never suspects it." Gabriel raised an eyebrow. "And the element of surprise may give us the edge."

"Give us the edge? Listen to you. You sound like a character out of one of your comic books." Vole swished his tale. "Don't let your guard down, Gabriel. Not for a moment. And be prepared for anything."

"There he is." Gabriel pointed to the sleek form of Mr. Wicked walking down the street toward his shop. "He's eating an ice cream cone?"

"Apparently so."Vole craned his fluffy neck as high as it could go. "Looks like chocolate."

"That jerk tried to make me eat worms," Gabriel huffed.

Mr. Wicked opened the door to Wicked Books and flicked on the lights.

"It's time, kid. Go get him."Vole nodded.

"Oh, it's on," Gabriel fumed as he began pedaling down the hill toward the store. "It is so on."

Chapter Forty Two:
A LITTLE GAME

Gabriel skidded to a stop in front of Wicked Books and dropped his bike in the dirt. Storming up to the front door, he knocked on the glass as hard as he could. After a moment, the deadbolt snapped open and the door swung wide. The inside of the store was completely dark. Gabriel found it hard to describe just how incredibly dark the room felt. It was as if light did not exist past the threshold of the front door and disappeared completely just a few steps beyond.

"Come in, Gabriel. I've been expecting you," Mr. Wicked's icy tones echoed out from within the pitch black chamber. Gabriel, who only a moment ago was ready to punch Mr. Wicked in the jaw, now found it nearly impossible to draw up the courage to take that first step.

Gabriel closed his eyes and thought about the night in the forest when the queen made him a knight. He thought about Vole and how bravely he fought off Mrs. Silverman at the farmhouse. Finally, he thought about, "Mom," he whispered to himself, and slowly took that first step into the bookstore.

Crossing the barrier into darkness, he felt a powerful chill creep up his leg. The room was freezing. Gabriel was certain that if he could see in the dark, he would be seeing steam rising off his breath. With a rattle and a bang, the front door slammed shut behind him, plunging Gabriel into utter and total darkness.

"You know, I saw you talking to the rodent up on the hillside a moment ago," Mr. Wicked continued. "I tried to warn you, lad. Those foxes are nothing but trouble. If you had listened to me, you would be living the life of a superhero right now, and your mother would be safe at home."

"Show yourself!" Gabriel demanded.

"What are you planning, Gabriel?" Mr. Wicked replied from the darkness. "I know you wouldn't have been chatting with your furry little friend if you weren't scheming something. I know you have your Riley: Ace of the Skies comic with you. Even though my powers are muted in this human husk, I can still sense that much. I know the comic is here in my store. So what's it going to be, Gabriel? What do you have in mind?"

The cold was seeping into every inch of Gabriel's being. "A game," Gabriel replied through chattering teeth.

"A game?"

"I thought you liked games."

"Of course I like games. In fact, I love games. And, contrary to folklore, I never lose at games. I am the Devil after all." And with that, the room was suddenly bathed in a creepy greenish blue glow. For the first time since he had entered the store, Gabriel could see. Standing in the middle of the room was Mr. Wicked. His piercing silvery-blue eyes were fixed on Gabriel. "So what sort of game should we play? And for what stakes?"

"I pick the game," Gabriel replied. It was so cold now that his entire body was shivering.

"Then, I pick the stakes," Mr. Wicked replied in a singsong manner. "If you win, I'll release your mother."

"And if I lose?"

"If you lose, then you... your comic book... and your mother will all be mine." Mr. Wicked spoke slowly and gnashed his teeth together hungrily on the word, mine.

"Agreed." Gabriel nodded.

Mr. Wicked looked slightly surprised at Gabriel's quick reply. "What game shall we play then?" he asked cautiously.

"One of your favorites." Gabriel smiled. He couldn't tell but he was certain his lips were turning blue. "Hot or Cold."

"Hot or Cold?"

"Yes. Vole has hidden my comic book somewhere in your store. If you can find it, then it's yours."

"Child's play!" Mr. Wicked replied triumphantly. "My prize will be firmly within my grasp in a matter of minutes. As will your eternal soul."

"Ready?" Gabriel asked.

"Ready." Mr. Wicked replied.

"Then, go." Gabriel nodded.

Mr. Wicked turned and slowly crept toward the silvery metal comic book racks. "It's obvious that you've hidden my prize somewhere among my own stock of tormented souls."

"You're ice cold." Gabriel shook his head and rubbed his arms to try and keep warm.

"I think you have that backwards, lad." Mr. Wicked laughed to himself as he slipped past the first row. On his face, Mr. Wicked wore the expression of a child on Christmas morning. "Where are you, Riley?" he called out playfully.

"Warmer," Gabriel said watching Mr. Wicked closely. The blue green glow was shimmering in the highlights of the metal racks as Mr. Wicked slinked deeper into his store.

"I am close. I can feel it," Mr. Wicked said as he walked past the third row.

"Warmer," Gabriel said as he slowly began to follow Mr. Wicked down the row, all the while watching him like a hawk.

"You really are a fool, Gabriel." Mr. Wicked chuckled. "I don't need you or your silly game. I can find that comic now all on my own. I can sense it. It calls to me. You see there's something about that comic book you don't know, Gabriel. And it will be the greatest gem in my collection!" Mr. Wicked passed the fourth row. Only two more to go.

"You're red hot," Gabriel added. Mr. Wicked stopped walking past the aisles and turned into the fifth row.

"I know." Mr. Wicked laughed again. He seemed to be in high spirits. "It's so close now, I can taste it." Mr. Wicked stopped in the middle of the fifth row. "I'm here. It's here somewhere. Riley is here!"

"You're burning up!" Gabriel shouted as he thundered forward toward Mr. Wicked. Slamming his shoulder into the metal rack, Gabriel knocked the entire comic book stand over. The first row toppled over and slammed into the second set of shelves, which in turn crashed into the third. The entire set of metal racks fell like enormous chrome dominos. All of the comic books tumbled from the racks, slipped free from their plastic bags, and spilled open across the tile floor.

"You fool! What are you doing?" Mr. Wicked shrieked.

"Fighting fire with fire!" Gabriel cried out as the room exploded in the biggest fireball anyone had ever seen.

Chapter Forty Three:
IRON AND WATER

The room exploded with fire. Flames filled every crack and crevice. In a flash, sparks spat out from under the front door and trickled up through the air vents. Gabriel closed his eyes as the fire engulfed him.

Within a moment, he felt himself falling though the air. The flames vanished as quickly as they had appeared.

Crashing to the ground, Gabriel heard a loud clanging sound as if someone had dropped a dozen garbage cans off the roof of a skyscraper. Rising to his feet, he felt strange. He was completely encased in some type of metal suit. There was padding, but not quite enough, and he could feel the cold steel rubbing against his back. On his head he now wore a form fitting iron mask. But in place of eye holes, a set of tiny view screens filled his vision.

"Oh my gosh," he exclaimed. "I'm in the Ironclad comic. I am Ironclad." Suddenly the screens lit up with red warning lights. Gabriel looked at the alarm. He was standing on top of his headquarters, the Iron Works that overlooked the city. Hovering in the air before him was Mr. Wicked, but he looked different. He was glowing with a brilliant yellow light, and he, too, was in a costume. His was bright yellow in color, and on his chest was the symbol of a black sun. "Mr. Wicked?" Gabriel asked out loud.

"Wicked? Who's that? Around here, the name's Solarius," Mr. Wicked roared. "I'm surprised you didn't recognize your arch enemy, Ironclad. Perhaps, you will remember this!" Mr. Wicked swung his arms wildly and a pair of lightning bolts shot from his fingertips. The bolts hit Gabriel square in the chest and knocked him backwards off the tower.

Gabriel heard the wind whisk past his helmet. He was falling fast. "Rocket boots activated," the mini computer in his helmet called out, and Gabriel felt his feet vibrating. He was instantly back in control. Gabriel was beginning to remember what it was like to be the Eternal Guardian, and things were starting to feel more natural.

Gabriel blasted into turbo and spun about in mid air. His tiny targeting computer locked on to Mr. Wicked. Racing up the side of his watchtower, he snapped loose one of the long radar antennae and swung it like a baseball bat as he roared past Mr. Wicked. With a crunch, the metal antenna caught Mr. Wicked square in the stomach and sent him flying like a homerun baseball. Gabriel watched as the yellow speck soared clear out of sight.

Touching down on the roof of the watchtower, Gabriel couldn't believe it. His plan was working! Here in the world of comic books, he was a pro. He knew every superhero. He knew all of their strengths and weaknesses. This was the one place where he might have a chance of beating Mr. Wicked, inside a comic book. But now that he was here, he wasn't certain what to do next. He hadn't thought that far ahead.

"So you want to play rough, do you?" Gabriel was jolted from his train of thought by the sight of Mr. Wicked (still dressed as Solarius) unleashing a barrage of lightning bolts at him. Gabriel made a great leap and rocketed away from Mr. Wicked as fast as he could. "You can't escape me that easily, lad," Mr. Wicked called out and began chasing Gabriel across the city skyline. "I love this new game of yours, Gabriel. Or should I say, Ironclad?" Mr. Wicked taunted. "But don't forget, I never lose at games."

Gabriel searched the city for some idea on how to stop Mr. Wicked, but nothing helped. Racing on, he looked everywhere frantically for some solution. Then he spotted it. The tunnel through the mountainside. Maybe he could lure Mr. Wicked inside the tunnel and crash the mountain down on him. "Catch me if you can, Solarius!" Gabriel shouted to Mr. Wicked as he folded his arms in tight and took off toward the tunnel like a shot.

"That's the spirit, lad! It will make my conquest all the more satisfying!" Mr. Wicked laughed as he raced behind Gabriel, flinging thunderbolts at his heels.

Gabriel swerved and dodged the blasts. His afterburners were on full power as he thundered over the afternoon traffic and entered the tunnel. The tunnel was packed with commuter cars.

There are too many people in here. I can't risk hurting anyone. Even in a comic book. Gabriel thought to himself as he raced over the cars. My plan isn't going to work. Maybe if there's something on the other side of this-

"What!" Gabriel cried out. The other end of the tunnel was missing! All Gabriel could see was a large fireball waiting for him where the tunnel exit was supposed to be. "I'm going too fast! I can't stop!"

Gabriel's view screens were all flashing red as he raced head first into the flames. Covering his face with his forearms, Gabriel braced himself for the impact. However, he did not crash. Nor did he burn. Just the opposite happened. Instead of smashing into the mountain wall, he found himself suddenly free of the armor and plunged into what felt like a cool, clear swimming pool.

Coming out of the other side of the flames, Gabriel was shocked. His Ironclad armor was gone, and instead, he was wearing a skintight blue uniform with the symbol of a Nautilus shell stitched in gold upon his chest. He was somewhere deep beneath the ocean's surface.

For a moment, he panicked. How could he be breathing? At first he didn't understand, but then it dawned on him where, and more importantly, who he was. Looking back, he saw the fiery porthole he had flown through quickly snuff itself out. Everything seemed darker here. Quieter. He didn't need to guess which comic he was in now. It was obvious that he was Oceanious, Warrior of Atlantis. But where was Mr. Wicked?

Gabriel peered through the murky sea water. A school of tiny orange fish scuttled past as he turned on his wrist light. The area around him lit up in a pale haze. He could see that he was near a coral reef, but that information didn't help him much.

Then Gabriel had a most troublesome thought. If he was Oceanious, then that would mean Mr. Wicked would be Oceanious' arch nemesis, The Mollusktron. A half squid, half robot that lurks in the darkest parts of the ocean. This is bad, Gabriel thought to himself. He began looking around for another portal of fire. He needed to get out of this comic, and fast!

Suddenly he felt something wrap tightly around his leg. It was a giant tentacle. Thick rubbery suckers caught his suit and held tight. With a lurch, the arm yanked Gabriel backward then pulled him through the water. Sand and shells flew up from the ocean floor making it nearly impossible to see. A large oily black shape emerged from the cloud of sand, followed by even more tentacles. The fat squishy arms wrapped themselves tightly around Gabriel's legs and chest. "Game over, Gabriel," Mr. Wicked's voice bubbled out from within the murky darkness. As the sand settled, Gabriel could see the compound eye lenses of the sea monster that was squeezing him. It was the Mollusktron.

"The name's Oceanious, pal," Gabriel replied as his breath was being crushed from his body.

The sea monster laughed. "Right," Mr. Wicked's voice echoed out across the sea floor. "Oceanious. Any last words, Oceanious?"

Gabriel found it nearly impossible to breathe. He had only one choice. If he really was Oceanious, then there was only one power he could call upon. Closing his eyes, he concentrated as hard as he could.

Help me, he thought to himself. I'm in danger. Please come to my aid, my friends. Gabriel grimaced and shut his eyes tightly as he listened to his own bones creaking under the strain of the sea monster's powerful arms.

Then a strange shape emerged from the inky darkness of the ocean floor. A large grey shape, the size of a submarine. Gabriel watched as the largest sperm whale he could have possibly imagined emerged from the dark depths and rammed the bulbous sea monster with its massive flat head. Gabriel heard Mr. Wicked cry out in pain, as the enormous whale turned and crashed into the Mollusktron a second time. The tentacles that were holding Gabriel loosened and spun through the water until they wrapped themselves tightly around the whale's body.

This was Gabriel's chance. Darting away as fast as he could, Gabriel swam straight for the surface. Maybe if he knew where in the world he was, he could think of some way to beat Mr. Wicked. Kicking with all of his might,

Gabriel watched as the Mollusktron and the whale slowly vanished within the dark void. Faint sparks lit up pockets of silt far beneath him as he swam upwards toward the bright sky above.

"Gabriel!" Mr. Wicked bellowed. "This isn't over!" Gabriel looked back down to see the red glow of the Mollusktron's robotic heart cutting through the gloom. Mr. Wicked was swimming fast toward the surface. He was heading on a collision course with Gabriel. "You will not escape me this time!" Gabriel swam as fast as he could. "The ocean will be your grave!" Mr. Wicked howled as his sleek, streamlined body shot to the surface.

Gabriel wasn't going to make it in time. Mr. Wicked was going to catch him again. Switching on his wrist light Gabriel searched in vain for something to use against Mr. Wicked. The ocean was a vast empty wasteland. No weapons. No more whales. Nothing but inky darkness. The only thing he could see was a faint light below him. It looked like some type of underground volcanic fissure in the ocean floor. No, Gabriel thought, not a hole, a porthole! A fiery portal out of here! But it was too far away to reach before Mr. Wicked would catch up with him. Gabriel closed his eyes and concentrated.

"I have you now! There are no foxes to save you down here!" Mr. Wicked spread out all eight of his thick tentacles and reached for Gabriel. There was a flash of silver, and Gabriel was gone. Mr. Wicked's rubbery tentacles became tangled around one another. "What!" Mr. Wicked growled and scanned the area with his laser eye.

"Better luck next time!" Gabriel yelled as he held tight to the dolphin's dorsal fin. The sleek silver swimmer had heard Gabriel's thoughts and arrived just in time. Mr. Wicked exploded in a roar that shook the ocean floor. "Faster, my friend," Gabriel whispered into the dolphin's ear. Like a tiny streak of lightning, Gabriel and the dolphin raced toward the underwater fireball with Mr. Wicked hot on their heels. As they approached the portal, Gabriel was stunned with how strange and beautiful the underwater fire looked. Gabriel closed his eyes and plunged face first into the cloud of cool flame. Gabriel knew he couldn't keep this up forever. Eventually, he would trip up and Mr. Wicked would have him. He needed to figure out a way to beat the Devil before it was too late.

In a flash, the fire was gone. The water was gone. Gabriel found himself sitting in a comfortable leather seat. In his hand, he held what felt almost like a videogame joystick. A pair of goggles covered his eyes, and a long scarf was draped around his neck. Clouds were racing past him as he looked out of the canopy of his fighter plane. "Oh my gosh," Gabriel whispered to himself. "I'm Riley, Ace of the Skies."

Chapter Forty Four:
RILEY'S LAST FLIGHT

Gabriel held the joystick tight and even. The sky was stunningly beautiful. He knew this comic book backwards and forwards. He figured he was flying somewhere over England. It was his best guess because he knew that Riley: Ace of the Skies number one was the issue where Riley teams up with the Royal Air Force and single handedly saves London from a squadron of Nazi bombers. So that would mean Mr. Wicked would probably be flying in a Nazi fighter plane; a Messerschmitt, no doubt.

Gabriel scanned the thick clouds for any sign of him. He couldn't let Mr. Wicked get the drop on him again like in the Oceanious comic. He needed to find Mr. Wicked first. He needed to have the element of surprise.

"Gabriel!" Mr. Wicked's voice howled over Gabriel's radio. "No more fun and games, boy! Now, I'm playing for keeps!" Gabriel felt his heart begin to race. His palms became moist, and they started to stick to the top of the joystick. He had never heard Mr. Wicked sound like that before. He sounded more like some type of wild animal than a man. "Gabriel! Where are you! Blast these clouds!"

Gabriel was about to switch on his radio and taunt Mr. Wicked, but decided against it. He didn't want to give away his position. He needed to stay silent, so Mr. Wicked wouldn't find him. Cruising high over the English countryside, Gabriel kept a stiff eye out for any sign of Mr. Wicked.

"Gabriel," Mr. Wicked's voice crackled over the tiny speaker. "I'll tell you what. You've given me a good run. In fact, you are one of the most worthy opponents I have faced in a long time. Why don't we call it a draw. Let's leave here together. I'll keep the comic, and you and your family may go free. What do you say, lad?" Mr. Wicked's voice was back to its usual icy tones. "Gabriel. I know you can hear me."

Gabriel's thumb rested on the intercom switch. Was this a trap? Should he say something? No. If Mr. Wicked knew where Gabriel was, then he wouldn't be wasting his time trying to make a deal. It was a trick.

"Going once!" Mr. Wicked's voice cut through the static. "Going twice!" Gabriel waited and kept his eyes on the clouds. "Gone! You foolish boy!" Gabriel listened as Mr. Wicked's voice turned wild once more. "So be it! You and your entire family will be mine! Just like your father!"

"Dad?" Gabriel stammered.

"Ah hah!" Mr. Wicked trumpeted. "I have you now!"

Gabriel heard the scream of a Messerschmitt slicing through the air as Mr. Wicked opened fire on him. A hail of bullets whisked past Gabriel's head. The shots found their mark, and they tore a hole through one of Gabriel's wings. Fuel began spraying from the bullet holes dousing his windshield and making it almost impossible to see. Gabriel gripped the hand crank and slid back the cockpit glass so he might see better. The cold winds over England ravaged Gabriel's skin, and his cheeks instantly began to burn. On top of that, his fuel gauge was slowly dropping.

Again, Mr. Wicked opened fire on Gabriel. Jerking the stick, Gabriel spun his fighter and began spiraling down toward the stark white cliffs of Dover.

"I'm Riley, I'm Riley, I'm Riley," he repeated to himself as he struggled to regain control of his plane. Mr. Wicked continued to pursue Gabriel. Again, he opened fire sending a steady stream of bullets straight at Gabriel. The shots missed Gabriel's wing by inches and carved a dark pattern on the white cliffs. "I'm Riley! Ace of the skies!" Gabriel screamed as loud as he could, and he pulled back on the stick with all of his might. With a roar, his fighter plane heaved back and raced almost vertically up the side of the cliff.

"What! That's impossible!" Mr. Wicked howled, and he attempted to follow, but his dive was too steep and he bailed out of his plane just moments before it crashed into the cliff wall, exploding upon impact. Gabriel watched as Mr. Wicked's parachute opened over the lush green English countryside.

With a sigh of relief, Gabriel checked his fuel gauge. He was still leaking fuel, but he figured he had enough to try and find the portal out of this comic book.

"It's not over yet, boy!" A monstrous roar echoed out from below Gabriel as a leathery winged monster flew up into sight. Gabriel twisted his neck around to see an enormous red demon soar up from the ground. "I never lose!" the beast bellowed. It was Mr. Wicked, Gabriel thought to himself. He's in his true form, like Vole talked about.

The demon raced up behind Gabriel and exhaled a blinding stream of fire at the tiny plane. Gabriel yanked the stick to avoid the blast, but the flames caught the tip of Gabriel's wing, igniting the stream of fuel. Gabriel's eyes went wide. He knew he only had a matter of seconds before the flames reached the fuel tanks and the entire plane would explode.

"You there, Riley?" A new voice crackled out over Gabriel's radio. "Flip the third switch on your left. The green one." Gabriel was curious who would be helping him, but right now he didn't want to argue. Glancing down he spotted the switch and flicked it. The steady stream of burning fuel was suddenly snuffed out. "You'll have to compensate now. Turn the center switch to go to your backup fuel reserve," again the mysterious voice crackled out over Gabriel's radio. Gabriel quickly turned the switch, and he felt something under his seat buckle. Although he didn't have much fuel left, his gauge stopped dropping and stayed steady. "Look out!" his radio hissed. Gabriel pulled back on the stick just missing another blast from Mr. Wicked's fiery mouth.

Gabriel picked up the receiver and clicked the button. "Who are you?" he asked.

"They call me the Sand Fox," the voice replied. "Now, get out of there. I'll finish off your friend."

Gabriel's mouth went completely dry. "Dad?" he exclaimed. Looking up, Gabriel spotted his father's jet fighter racing out of the sun.

"Fire one!" The voice called out, and a pair of missiles streaked off the side of his fighter jet. Gabriel watched in awe as the rockets found their target, striking Mr. Wicked square in the chest. The beast lost control and tumbled wildly through the air until it crashed head first into the sea. A magnificent cloud of steam rose up from where Mr. Wicked fell. "Now, hurry up and follow me. We're running out of time!" Gabriel's father's jet peeled off and headed straight toward one of the burning portals. Although his plane was much slower and older than his father's, Gabriel followed his dad through the portal. Everything grew bright as the plane melted away, the blue sky vanished, and Gabriel's feet gently came to rest on the ground.

That would be the very last time Gabriel ever saw Mr. Wicked.

Chapter Forty Five:
SAYING GOODBYE

The bright light dimmed and Gabriel found himself standing in a dark room with a pile of disheveled comic books resting underfoot. He was back inside Wicked Books, however the sickly green light was now all gone. In its place, moonlight streamed in through the windows and all was calm. Beneath his feet was the Ironclad comic he had first fallen into when all of the comic books spilled open, but now there was no fire, no magic, just a peaceful evening in a quiet old shop. It was as if he had woken up from a strange and terrible nightmare.

"That was some pretty good flying back there, kiddo."

Gabriel knew that voice. He turned around to see his father standing before him. He was still dressed in his flight jumpsuit. In his hand, he held the Riley: Ace of the Skies comic book. "Dad? Is that really you?" Gabriel asked.

"Yes, it is." Mr. Woods smiled and knelt down. Gabriel ran up and threw his arms around his father. The two exchanged a long hug.

"I miss you, Dad," Gabriel said.

"I know, son. I miss you, too." Mr. Woods replied as he picked the plastic bag up off the floor and slipped the comic book neatly inside. He then folded the top over and closed it tight. "I think your friend will have a tough time getting out of this one," his father smiled as he held the Riley comic up to the moonlight.

"So he's stuck in there. Right, Dad?" Gabriel asked.

"Yup. Like a rat." Mr. Woods nodded, and he handed the comic back to Gabriel.

"Your comic book." Gabriel stammered looking at the book in the transparent bag. "I kept it safe."

"I know you did. You did a great job taking care of it for me."

"I miss you, Dad. Mom misses you. I wish you were still with us." Gabriel sighed.

"But I am with you. I'm always with you, Gabriel. That's why I was able to help you. You never gave up on me, and I'll never give up on you, or your mother. We will always be together, even if you can't see me."

"I love you, Dad," Gabriel finally choked as he threw his arms around his father one last time.

"I love you too, son," Mr. Woods whispered. Gabriel felt his grip on his father become weaker and weaker as Mr. Woods gradually vanished from sight. Eventually, he disappeared completely, leaving Gabriel all alone in the cold empty shop.

Chapter Forty Six:
NOVEMBER

"Are you certain about this, Master Woods?" Mr. Higby stood on the far side of the front counter. He was looking up at Gabriel who was sitting on an old wooden stool. "This is quite a rare comic book. Possibly one of the rarest in the world. I will not be inclined to return it if you get cold feet on the sale," Mr. Higby squeaked as he cast a hungry eye on Gabriel's copy of Riley: Ace of the Skies. The comic was resting on the counter top, still sealed up in the same plastic bag from Halloween.

"I'm sure. There's just one condition of me selling this comic book to you," Gabriel replied.

"And what would that be?" Mr. Higby asked cautiously.

"I want you to promise me you will never, ever, open it. Not even to read. If you can promise me that, then it's yours."

Mr. Higby's face instantly lit up. "Oh, yes. I can absolutely promise you that. In fact..." Mr. Higby stopped talking and popped his briefcase open on the glass counter. A puff of cool steam rose up from within and hit Gabriel in the face. Looking into the case, Gabriel saw a strange device with several metal cylinders and what appeared to be a transparent plastic vault. "You see, the moment you sell me that comic book, I plan on permanently sealing it away in this climate controlled case. The book is quite old and rare, after all. Not meant to be handled too much or too often or else I'm certain it would fall apart. In fact, I'm a little suspicious of how you were able to take such good care of it for so long, not to mention how you were able to purchase this store. You are still in grade school after all." Mr. Higby's hooked nose whistled as he spoke.

"Oh, this store." Gabriel looked around the comic book shop. It had taken him a few weeks to clean it all up and fix all the damage from his fight with Mr. Wicked. Fortunately, he was able to sell off a few comics from Mr. Patrick's secret stash to pay for it all, but now Wicked Books was his. Lock, stock and barrel. "You could say an old friend helped me out." Gabriel smiled.

"Yes, I see," Mr. Higby replied. "Actually, I don't see. I have no idea what you are talking about. So, do we have a deal?" Mr. Higby held out his right hand for Gabriel to shake.

"Deal," Gabriel replied, and he vigorously shook Mr. Higby's hand. Gabriel's grip was so strong that the tiny man was knocked off balance a bit.

"Wise deal, young Master Woods," Mr. Higby replied as he unfolded his check book and wrote Gabriel a check on the spot for fifty thousand dollars.

"I'll take that, thank you," Mrs. Woods entered the comic book shop and plucked the check from Mr. Higby's fingertips as she passed. "Hey there, kiddo. I brought you a late lunch," Mrs. Woods chimed as she plopped a brown paper bag on the counter next to a large stack of comics.

"Thanks, Mom," Gabriel smiled as he tore open the bag. "Aw. Tuna again?"

"Eat up. It's good for you," Mrs. Woods replied as she picked up the stack of comic books and slowly began searching for their rightful places on the shelves. Gabriel peeled back the plastic wrap and began gnawing on the hard crusty corner of the sandwich.

Mr. Higby took the Riley: Ace of the Skies comic and slipped it into the plastic case. He then sealed the latches tightly, and turned the climate switch on the side of the briefcase to eleven. "Then, I assume, that concludes our business for the day. It was a pleasure dealing with you, Master Woods." Mr. Higby tipped his hat to Gabriel and skipped out the door hugging his briefcase as he went.

"There goes a happy gent." Vole smiled from his seat in the corner.

"So, Vole. What does this all mean now?" Gabriel asked as he shook the bottom of the lunch bag forcing an unbaked potato to tumble out onto the counter. "Mom!" Gabriel groaned. "You grabbed a potato instead of an apple again!"

"My bad," Mrs. Woods replied from somewhere behind the backmost shelf.

"Well, according to mother," Vole began, "I hear my family is about to move again. To someplace called Central Park in the far away land of Manhattan. Apparently, the poor town is about to have a rather nasty fox infestation." Vole smiled.

"So, you are going to follow Mr. Higby?" Gabriel asked. "You're leaving me? But you know, Vole, you're one of the closest things I've ever had to a best friend."

"I know, Gabriel, and I've come to think of you as a little brother. However, duty calls and I must stay with my family, just as you must stay with yours." Vole smiled a sad sort of smile and held out his hand for Gabriel to shake. Instead, Gabriel jumped off his stool and gave Vole a big hug, then shook his hand. "Don't worry, Gabriel. I'm certain you and I will meet again. You are a Royal Knight of the Foxes. That is a rare thing, indeed."

"Yeah," Gabriel replied. "I'll still miss all of you. Thank you again for all your help. And please thank your mother for me when you see her again."

"I will," Vole replied. He then held up a hand full of comic books and raised an eyebrow to Gabriel.

"On the house." Gabriel winked, and Vole placed the comics into his satchel.

"Goodbye for now, Gabriel Woods, defender of the forest." Vole nodded.

"Goodbye, Vole, prince of the forest." Gabriel returned the nod. And with a turn of his heel, Vole exited the store and vanished down the street.

"Who was that?" Mrs. Woods asked.

"Just an old friend," Gabriel replied.

"Oh," Mrs. Woods said as she examined Mr. Higby's check. "You know, I was thinking. It's been pretty crazy around here lately. Storms and foxes and bears and junk. I think we may need some help around the house. What do you think about our getting a dog? You know? Someone to scare away monsters and eat the left over broccoli you hide in your napkin? That sort of stuff. What do you say, kiddo?"

Gabriel turned to his mother and smiled. "I think that idea is totally wicked!"

THE END

Christopher DeSantis was born in Boston Massachusetts in 1973. A noted filmmaker, his work has appeared in both national and international film festivals. He has received several awards for his films including the Nickelodeon: Nicktoons Creator award for his animated short film, Fowl Play. Wicked Books marks Christopher's first publication in fiction.

www.ingramcontent.com/pod-product-compliance
Lightning Source LLC
Chambersburg PA
CBHW052132170626
46812CB00004B/1375